INTRODUCING
PARRI

JANET LAMBERT

Cover: Based on an award-winning photo by Bruce Geist, West High School, Phoenix, Arizona, 1969 Scholastic/Kodak Photography Awards

SCHOLASTIC BOOK SERVICES

NEW YORK · TORONTO · LONDON · AUCKLAND · SYDNEY

This book is sold subject to the condition that it shall not be resold, lent, or otherwise circulated in any binding or cover other than that in which it is published—unless prior written permission has been obtained from the publisher—and without a similar condition, including this condition, being imposed on the subsequent purchaser.

Copyright © 1962 by Janet Lambert. This edition is published by Scholastic Book Services, a division of Scholastic Magazines, Inc., by arrangement with E. P. Dutton & Co., Inc.

2nd printing......................................January 1970

Printed in the U.S.A.

For Folly

My dear little French poodle friend, who like Peppi before her, is always faithful and loving no matter how long I sit at my typewriter.

AND

For Tupper

My pleasant gray tiger cat, who while not so faithful, comes in now and then to stir things up.

CHAPTER 1

"Are you sure you'll be all right?" Josh MacDonald leaned across the seat of the car to look at his daughter standing on the sidewalk.

Reason told him she was much too young to be left alone on Fifth Avenue, even though she would only go into one store to make one purchase, then take a taxicab to his office. But New York was such a tremendous city; and Parri, in a navy-blue pleated skirt, with her round school hat perched on top of her head, with her brown curls blowing against her young cheeks in the brisk fall wind, looked like the schoolgirl she was.

"Oh, Daddy, of *course!*" Parri was impatient to begin her day. It wouldn't be much, but at least it would be a change from the usual dull Saturdays in the country. "Mums and I've rehearsed it a dozen times," she said, repeating everything once more so he would drive on. "I'm to go straight up to the Junior Department and ask Miss Heatheridge to show me the two coats Mums had laid away. Then Miss Heatheridge is to come back downstairs with me and stand faithfully by while the doorman calls me a cab. Then, if she likes the kind of face the driver has, I'm to get in and give him your office address. Oh, Daddy, it's all so simple! I'm not a *baby*. I'm fifteen years old and . . ."

"You're fourteen and a few days," her father interrupted; and then he sighed. "I wish I didn't have an important meeting that I can't put off," he said. "I have, though, so I'll get back to the office as soon as I can, and we'll go somewhere nice for lunch."

"All right, Daddy." Parri took a step backward, then stopped to smile at him. His dear craggy face looked so unsure and troubled. His kind gray eyes that were his only handsome feature were filled with the same misgiving which had twice made him decide to stop production of a play he had bought, even though he had begun rehearsals. "Look, Daddy," she leaned closer to say, before he could drive off to a parking lot and postpone whatever meeting he had, to come back and take her in tow again. "I know exactly what to do, so stop worrying. Mums planned it this way."

"You're right, she did." Josh took one more long look at her before he slid back under the wheel.

Parri's mother had got loose in New York City once, he remembered ruefully, when she was only a little older than Parri, and had managed to rescue a well-known actress. She had been bitten by the acting bug at an early age, and now she was a star. But most actresses didn't go about falling off curbs, he reasoned, for starry-eyed girls to pick up; and furthermore, Parri already knew dozens of them. And even furthermore, she was a normal kid who thought her famous parents were just everyday people like her uncles and aunts. And she didn't like being in school plays, and hated New York, and Miss Heatheridge would look after her.

"All right," he said, starting the motor. "I'll be expecting you at the office in a little over an hour. One o'clock. If I should happen to be late, sit down and read." And he took his foot off the brake of his foreign sports car.

"I will," Parri promised, little dreaming that history has a way of, if not exactly repeating itself, following a familiar pattern.

She didn't wait to watch him move out into traffic, but turned and hurried through the glass door a doorman held open for her. She would have liked to hover over the jewelry counter—not to buy any of the glittering necklaces and bracelets, because she had the authority to charge only one coat, but just to pretend. And the gloves looked so inviting. There were evening gloves, daytime gloves—all of such beautiful soft kid and suede that she hastily stuffed her own serviceable pigskins into her jacket pocket. An elevator was going up, and she stepped into it and out again on the third floor, still coveting all the beautiful accessories she had seen. Someday she would have them. Someday, she told herself, she would be far more famous than her mother. Penny Parrish, winner of an Oscar and the best actress on Broadway, could be *nothing* compared to Parrish MacDonald, toast of the world.

"Oh, there you are," Miss Heatheridge hurried toward her to say. "I've been expecting you. Your mother just phoned, and you're to call your Aunt Carrol if anything goes wrong about meeting your father."

"Yes, I know," Parri answered, her big brown eyes changing back from shining orbs to just brown eyes. "She's having lunch at Antonio's. Mums told me."

"Your mother thinks of everything," Miss Heatheridge commended proudly, nodding her graying head. "I don't see how she does it, busy as she is. Why, she even sent me two tickets to her last play, because it was sold out for months, and I couldn't buy any. Come along, let's see which of the coats you like. You sit here on this sofa while I bring them out."

The prospect was not inviting, but Parri sat down. Perhaps at last, she hoped, after fourteen years of wearing straight belted-in-the-back reefers, her mother might have realized that she was growing up. Perhaps these coats might be more teen-agish than childish.

But no. Miss Heatheridge was returning, bearing two more of the same old model. One was cinnamon brown with a checked wool lining, the other navy blue, wool-lined in red. One had bone buttons, the other brass, and each had a neat little belt to pinch in its back.

Parri studied them. They were childish and exactly what her little cousin Carli wore; and if the navy blue were shorter and had no belt, and buttoned to the right instead of the left, it would be a duplicate of the one her little brother Joshu went off to Sunday school in.

"Don't you have anything more—more sophisticated?" she asked. "My mother said I don't have to take either of these," she explained, "if I find something I like better."

It wasn't exactly true; so, instead of looking up at the astonished saleswoman, she let her gaze rest on a mannequin that wore a red coat trimmed and lined with shining black fur. "Something like that," she said, pointing.

"That?" Miss Heatheridge couldn't believe her ears. "Why, that's frightfully expensive and far too old for you," she said.

"I'd like to try it on."

Parri was still dizzy from all the glitter she had seen displayed on the main floor. Heretofore she had always come into this exclusive woman's shop with her mother, and they had raced through it as if they wore blinders and were hitched to a sulky. "I've always liked red," she said, and watched Miss Heatheridge disrobe the mannequin down to a short jeweled sheath.

The coat was too large, but a smaller size from the stock room fitted Parri as if it had been tailored for her. "I love it," she said, standing before a triple mirror and posing with her hands in her pockets, not knowing that the fur lining and stand-up collar and great wide cuffs were Hudson seal.

The coat did have four big black buttons on the front, she told herself, making it the double-breasted kind her mother always selected. But instead of having a silly little belt across the back, it swung free from the shoulders and widened into such a flare that the black fur showed when she twirled around. "I'll take it," she decided suddenly. "I'll just wear my jumper under it because it's rather warm today, and you can send my jacket."

Her funny round hat looked ridiculous topping off such a sophisticated coat, so she tossed it on the sofa too, and asked, "Where do I sign?"

"My goodness, you look just like your mother in this!" Miss Heatheridge exclaimed, flustered. "Shall we call her and ask if you may have it?"

"Of course not. I'll just sign the sales slip."

Parri was completely carried away by her sudden graduation from childhood to young womanhood, and she wanted to get out of there before Miss Heatheridge came to and insisted on putting in a call to Round Tree Farm up on the Hudson. "It's quite all right," she said, copying her mother's voice—the one Penny Parrish sent across the footlights, not the one Mrs. MacDonald would use to shriek, "For heaven's sake, Miss Heatheridge, get her out of it as fast as you can! Tell her it's either the brown or blue, or *nothing!*"

But Miss Heatheridge was still doubtful. Not that Mrs. MacDonald's charge account would be overburdened by the cost of the coat, she was sure, but would Mrs. MacDonald ever come in again to buy from her? And would Penny Parrish ever see that she got tickets to another play, or invite her backstage, or autograph her most recent photograph? Losing the prestige of knowing Penny Parrish was almost worse than losing the MacDonald account. Then she saw the floor manager off in the distance and decided to take the unfortunate matter to him. "You wait here a minute," she said. "I'll be right back."

Parri's watchful eyes followed her along the thick carpet to the door of a small cubicle that was the manager's office. There was sure to be a telephone in there, and her mother was sure to be home. The coat was so beautiful. And it did make her look so—so *glowing*. Everybody would love it, once they saw it, and her father would be terribly proud to take such a lovely young lady to lunch. Of course he would.

Miss Heatheridge's sales book lay on the sofa, a pencil tucked into it, ready and waiting, so Parri bent down and carefully wrote her name where she had seen her mother sign hers. Then she picked up her brown battered purse that had spent more time on the floor of her school bus than on her lap—and looked it—and took off toward the elevators.

Her heart was thumping so hard that when a car opened its doors she plunged in, not caring whether it went up or down. She had her coat. Of course she needed gloves, she thought, stroking the fur on her three-quarter sleeves—long black suede ones instead of the pigskin horrors she had left in her jacket pocket. And if her purse clashed in a cheap, vulgar way, perhaps she could carry it under her arm and no one would see it. Her patent-leather Sunday pumps had a hint of a heel and were as shiny as her new fur. She would do, she told herself, because many well-dressed women are careless about their gloves and purses and never wear hats.

Fortunately the elevator was going down, and it let her out while Miss Heatheridge was frantically punching the signal button. Parri walked through the store, eyes straight ahead until she passed the purse department. If she could find something for two ninety-eight, she thought, looking into the glass cases, she would still have enough of her five dollars left to pay her taxi fare. But there was nothing under fifteen dollars, so she pursued her important way outside.

The doorman didn't recognize her. A girl had gone in, a young lady came out, so he hurried off to put an elderly, mink-decked woman into her limousine, unaware of Miss Heatheridge charging up behind him, looking like a dispirited bloodhound that had lost the scent.

Parri had decided to walk, and had turned left along Fifth Avenue. Buying the coat had taken no more than twenty-five minutes, so she still had thirty-five left in which to stroll along and show off. Someday, she thought, swishing so the back of her coat would swing out and show its fur lining, people would turn, stop, and gaze after her. "There she is!" they would cry. "Let's run and get her autograph!" But nobody noticed her now. A few stock girls off for their lunch hour did look enviously at her fine red coat, and a man wondered how the kid stood it with a fur collar up around her chin on such a warm day.

Parri knew where she was going. She would walk down the avenue to Forty-second Street, then across town to a drugstore where, so her mother and father had often said, hopeful young actors gathered. She would watch them. Some would be studying their scripts perhaps, some would be talking about the parts they hoped to get; and she would feel as her mother said she had when she was poor and struggling and trying to land a part. This was the drugstore where Penny Parrish had started her career, she told her reflection in a shop window, and where Parrish MacDonald in her fine, fur-lined coat would enter like a rocket.

Parri's knowledge of rockets was limited to the programs she had seen on TV, but they were studying metaphors and similes in school, and she thought this was a simile, and a good one at that.

She found the place crowded. The walk had taken longer than she had expected it to, and the noon crowd of young clerks, stenographers, and a few legitimate young actors had all the booths. A stool at the counter was the best she could do, and she got that only when a pimply boy crumpled his paper napkin into his empty milk glass and slid off.

"Let me see," Parri said uncertainly to a waitress who swiped a sponge in a circle on the counter. "I'm having lunch later with a producer, so I think I'd better just have some celery and radishes and—well, a bowl of clear soup."

"We don't have any of that."

The girl who spoke wasn't so many years older than Parri, but she seemed so. She looked tired and disgusted with the whole business. "Okay," Parri said. "Bring me a cheeseburger and a Coke."

"Coming up."

Parri was where she wanted to be, and she swung around on her stool to look the place over. It was dull. She couldn't see what her mother had found so fascinating about it, or why young actors would want to sit for hours on end in the skimpy booths. And it was dirty. The floor was littered with cigarette butts and paper straws, and the tables were smeared. I'll never know why Mums was so keen about it, she thought disgustedly. Then the girl on her left spoke to her.

"You're putting your sleeve in the mustard," she said, having noted Parri's expensive coat. And she asked curiously, "Are you in the theater?"

"Oh, thank you. Yes, well—not yet, but I hope to be," Parri answered, scrubbing away with her paper napkin. "Are you?"

"Sometimes." The girl looked older than Parri, and she said, "I do modeling for Corridon—it's the best photographic modeling agency, you know. You can see me in *Harper's* and *Seventeen* any time you pick up a magazine, and in catalogues too. And I've had TV commercials and two parts in a legit. That means the legitimate theater," she added, sure that Parri was too green to know. "How old are you?"

"I'm . . ." Parri looked at the bleached head beside her. Its shaggy cut almost obscured a pair of beautiful blue eyes, and too much lipstick almost ruined a mouth that was delicately curved. "I'm sixteen," she said, plunging.

"Wish I were. Fifteen, that's me. I'm getting too big for the kid ads and not old enough for the deb stuff. But I get by. You live uptown or down?"

"In the country." Parri knocked off words in the abbreviated style that seemed correct in here, and asked, "You?"

"On West Eighth Street. I come from a long line of theater people," the girl offered.

"You *do?*" Parri put breathless awe into her simple remark and got full return for it, for the girl said more expansively:

"Sure. Mom was in musical comedy—just the chorus—until Pop died and she had to get a steady job to support us kids. But my Uncle Ben plays regularly in a TV soap opera and coaches me on the side, and another uncle was one of the kids in *Life with Father* until he got too big. Now he's out in Hollywood and doing all right. My sister was in a couple of plays too, but she got tired of it and got married. It helps you to have an acting background."

"I suppose it does."

Parri watched the girl bend over her sandwich again, wondering how to recapture her attention. This must be the sort of thing her mother had done years ago, except that her mother had been nineteen, and an eager young stage manager named Josh MacDonald had usually sat on the stool next to her. "What's your name?" she asked.

"Stage or real?"

"Both, I guess."

"Well, it's like this." The girl laid her sandwich back on her plate and carefully wiped her mouth before she said, "I got born Mary Schultz—Mary for my grandma and Schultz courtesy of Pop. But Mom was always billed as May Showers, so I changed. I'm April Showers."

"April. It's a pretty name," Parri said, trying it again. "April. I like it. It sounds so young and—and fresh and lovely."

"Well, thanks." April looked around again with more interest. Miss Gotrocks wasn't exactly stupid, so she asked, "What's yours?"

"Mine?" Parri hesitated. MacDonald might get

17

by, but coupled with Parrish it would be a dead giveaway to anyone who knew as much about the theater as April seemed to. "I'm in the same fix you were," she said carefully, searching frantically for a name that would be as alluring as April Showers. And she stalled for time by biting into the sloppy bun that had been set before her and chewing slowly. Carrol—Tippy—Susan. Those were her aunts' names. Ellie, Hope, Beth, Althea, were friends at school. "What would you think," she asked, blindly plucking one like drawing a number from a raffle bowl, "of Carol? And perhaps Gay. Carol Gay. I know a family named Gay, and it sounds like happy singing, don't you think? And I know a family named Sweet. Carol Sweet."

"Not bad. Is Carol your real name?" April asked.

"It's my middle name." Parri was honest about that, at least, and she added, "It's *C-a-r-r-o-l* with a double *r*, but I wouldn't have to use the extra *r* if it spoiled the singing sound; and my last name's MacDonald, which doesn't match very well."

"Okay, Carol you are. We'll have to think about the last name. I believe I like Gay better." The luncheonette space was more than crowded now, and April turned to two girls who were pushing against them, saying good-naturedly, "Hey, take it easy. You'll get our seats when we're ready to leave, so don't shove. You should have come earlier."

"Oh, my goodness, what time is it?" Parri cried. Her watch was broken, as usual, so she leaned over to look at April's. "Why, it's a quarter to one!" she gasped. "I have to go!" And the girl behind her almost pushed her off the stool.

"So do I." April picked up her check and carefully counted out the exact seventy-five cents for her lunch, then laid a nickel on the counter. "I'm supposed to be over at the Gantry at one," she said, "to try out for a part. It's no good for me, but a theatrical agency's sending me and they'll check on it. Want to come along for the ride?"

"You mean—to a *theater?*"

"Sure. If you're trying to break into the game, you ought to see how it's done. You can sit off in the wings somewhere and watch."

"Dear me." Parri hated to give up her new friend, but where could she tell her father she had been? And what if they should walk along and meet him? He was always popping in and out of theaters, and the manager of the Gantry was a friend of his. What if his conference was being held there? "Oh, dear me," she repeated, while April moved the mustard farther away from her sleeve. "Do you think I could?"

"Why not? All the kids go with each other." April misunderstood the meaning of Parri's "could," and explained, "Sometimes we cut each other's throats, but you won't bother me because we aren't the same type and I kind of like you." Then, reaching down at her feet for a patent-leather hatbox, she added with no change of tone, "All right, girls, start your countdown."

"I'd like to pay for your lunch," Parri said gratefully, sliding off her stool and finding it occupied before the full folds of her coat had left it. She knew it wasn't ethical to make such an offer in the lower bracket of theatrical professionals, but she wanted to do something for this wonderful girl who was generously ready to help her start a career. April was a true friend. The truest she had ever known. And while she pushed both checks through the wicket in the grill of the checker's booth, she forgot she was incognito and asked eagerly, "Will you come out to the country and visit me sometime?"

"If I'm not working."

Visiting in the country sounded dull to April, but Parri asked eagerly, "Where can we write to invite you?"

"At Corridon's, I guess. I'm always in and out of there, getting modeling jobs, you know, and I usually eat my lunch here."

They were squeezed into one segment of the revolving door and, protecting her coat as they spun through, Parri had to wait until they were outside to say, "But my mother will have to write a note to your mother so she'll know we're the right sort of people and will let you come. Where should she send it?"

"Corridon's. Mom's never home much, so send it to Corridon's." April didn't bother to explain that she and her mother lived in a theatrical boardinghouse where everybody's mail was well pawed over before the addressee received it, because the letter didn't matter anyway. She would go or not as she liked.

"This is fun, isn't it?" Parri said, as they pushed their way through the endless stream of people who always crowd Broadway. "I've never done anything like this before."

"For Pete's sake, why not?"

"Because . . ." They were passing the Astor Hotel, where Parri's mother, one bright football Saturday afternoon just like today, had managed to get lost from her brother David, his date, and hers. Out she had rushed, a country girl hunting for a subway that would take her to the stadium. Then, smack-bang, she had rescued Miss Ware and ended up spending the whole afternoon and evening in a theater. Exactly like me, Parri thought, feeling a sharp twinge of conscience because it was her father she was abandoning, not just a date. Then she realized that April was still waiting for her answer. "Because I never had a city friend before," she said. And feeling suddenly happy and expansive, she confided, "I was supposed to have lunch with my father, and I didn't tell you the truth about my age. I'm only fourteen."

"I sort of wondered." It didn't matter to April. She rarely told the truth about her own age. She could be twelve or twenty, whichever best suited the job she wanted, so she only said, "We turn here," and shoved them both around the corner. "That's the theater down there—the second one on this side of the street."

"Oh." Parri peered intently along the block, looking not at the theater but for a tall, thin, rangy man who never wore a hat on his thick black hair.

"And since you don't know what you're getting into," April went on, "I'll brief you. You don't know much about theaters, do you?" she stopped to ask.

"Well, I've been in a lot of them," Parri answered, hedging, "but not like this."

"We don't go in through the lobby. We go down this alley to the stage door," April said. "Remember that. Actors always use the stage door."

"Thanks." Parri was ashamed to seem so grateful; and she took a good peek down the alley before she turned into it. The way was clear, so she slipped her arm through April's and let her coat swing jauntily as they walked along, the hatbox bumping between them.

"I've got a modeling job at two, and I can't be

late," April said, when they reached a heavy door and Parri was tugging it open. "This run-through won't take me very long, and I'll guide you back to Broadway if you want me to."

"Oh, I know where to go." Parri understood about the hatbox now. It held make-up and shoes and accessories. She had seen pictures of pretty models carrying them, and she was impressed because April really was the professional she had claimed to be. "I'll just watch you and hope you get the part," she said, "then I'll hustle off and meet my father."

CHAPTER 2

THE DARKENED THEATER SMELLED SO FAMILIAR. It was like dozens of others Parri had known, but as the door slammed shut she listened to April explain, "That's the call board over there on the wall, and the actors hang their dressing-room keys on those hooks. A man usually sits here by the door to keep strange people from barging in."

"Oh," Parri said, in well-feigned ignorance.

"And the actors' dressing rooms are in here," April went on, leading the way into a vast, dark cavern. "That's the star's, right there, but everybody else has to go up those stairs."

"Oh," Parri said again, looking where April pointed.

She knew that dressing room by heart, every foot of it. At four, she had had a little table and chair in one corner of it, with coloring books and crayons, modeling clay and colored beads in a bag, all kept in a drawer in her mother's make-up table. Joshu had had a highchair; and sometimes on Wednesdays or Saturdays, between the matinee and evening performance, a waiter from a restaurant would wheel in a table covered with a white cloth and silver dishes, and the whole MacDonald family would have dinner around it. Penny Parrish had hated anything that robbed her of time with her children, so Joshu had sat in his highchair and Parri on a spindly stool with the telephone directory on it, and afterward their father had taken them home.

"It certainly is dark in here," she said, looking through a maze of scenery to a stage where a naked electric bulb hung on a cord.

"*Cupid's Angel*'s playing here," April said, "and they've got the first-act flats set up. They don't want to take everything down because *Delayed Honeymoon*'s only used it for try-outs. Follow me, and sit on one of those chairs over there. If you don't say anything, nobody'll know you're here."

"Okay."

Parri, who had spent the last ten minutes in watchful peering, took a cautious look at the stage. She had never seen the young man who was mulling over some manuscripts at a table under the light. He was probably the assistant something-or-other, she decided. So she fumbled her way to a folding chair that couldn't adequately accommodate both her and her voluminous coat, and with as little commotion as possible laid her purse on the floor. April marched straight into the lighted space and introduced herself.

The part she was handed looked very thin to Parri. Accustomed to seeing typewritten pages stapled inside blue covers, she knew there couldn't be many speeches on these few, but she did hope April would do well with what little she had. And she hoped the young whatever-he-was wouldn't be influenced by April's too-blond mane and too-red lipstick. April, with her high heels and patent-leather hat case, didn't look like a twelve-year-old. But neither had Mrs. MacDonald from Round Tree Farm looked like a fashion designer when she began rehearsing her last play, Parri told herself, but, by golly, she had turned into one.

April's voice was too high. Parri hadn't noticed it as being high while they had talked together, but now it kept rising higher and higher. It screeched. It went "Er-uh-eeee," and then it screeched out words like a piece of chalk rubbed over glass. Perhaps that was what the young man wanted it to do, but Parri didn't think so; and she kept pressing her hands down on her knees, hard, as if that would bring it down. And then the reading was over. April had finished her speeches, and she and the young man were just standing there looking at each other.

"Thank you," he said, reaching for the part. And then, showing how new he was in show business, he repeated courteously, "Thank you very much. You read very well, and we'll let your agency know as soon as we've finished all the casting." Then he looked at Parri, half hidden in the gloom. "What agency sent you?" he asked.

"I just came." Parri was surprised to be discovered. "I just came with April," she said. "You know, for the ride."

"Do you want to read?"

"No." Parri did, but it wouldn't be fair to say so. She was sure she could do a lot better as the poor child who wanted so much to be adopted than April had, but it wouldn't be fair. This was April's chance. "Thank you," she said, "but—well, no." And she stood up.

She was a bright splotch of red in the dim light, and her very young face looked wistfully out of a black collar. It looked lonely and eager, yet timidly afraid. The young man, James Wayne, on his first big job as assistant director, couldn't know it was Penny Parrish's daughter who stood there, turning herself into Maggie Smith who was nobody's child. "You're very kind," Parri said softly, in the lonely voice April should have used, "but we'd better go now."

"Wait just a minute."

April had already retrieved her hatbox and was impatient to leave. She had sensed that she was too brittle for the part, and she asked, "Coming, kid?"

"Yes." Parri groped around for her purse in a helpless, Maggie-like way, as James Wayne walked over to her.

"How about giving it a try?" he suggested. "You *are* an actress, aren't you?"

"Oh, yes." Parri knew she was acting a part right now, but she repeated honorably, "I just came with April."

"And I'm leaving." April came over too. "Don't cry in your soup," she said, shrugging. "If I cut my own throat, so what? It's not your funeral."

She turned away, but Parri clutched her. "I don't want the part, April," she said, hanging onto the sleeve of April's shaggy coat that wasn't fur but looked a little like it. "My mother—my father . . . I mean—they'll help you, April. I promise!"

"Okay. Be seeing you."

April was gone. Her first true friend was gone before she had really become a friend.

Parri stood under the naked bulb and wished with all her heart that she had never found and lost April. But, unconsciously, she stood there looking like Maggie, who had lost so many chances in her short life. "All right," she said, flinging her purse at the chair, then going over to settle her coat on it as if it were the only precious possession she had left, the way Maggie would do, "I guess I'd like to try the part now."

Her accent, when she began to read, was slurred and amateurish, but she had something. Word endings that were lost, or unexpected pauses, were covered by gestures of apology. She was a pitiful little Maggie in a jumper and wilted white blouse; and if anyone could be said to sidle when she moved, Parri sidled like a crab drawn irresistibly toward the devouring light of a bonfire. She was Maggie, all right, James Wayne decided. In need of coaching, sure, but so honest and pitiful that, with help, she would reach across the footlights and tear pieces out of hundreds of hearts.

"All right, that's enough," he said, when she was exhausted from doing the short scene over and over. "You'll do. What's your name?"

"Huh?" Parri came to with a start and blinked at him, trying to forget Maggie and remember her father who was no doubt pacing the floor in a high office building. "It's—well, it's Carol," she said.

"Carol what?"

"Well. . . ." *Carol* had been written blackly on a piece of paper with a ballpoint pen and, fascinated, she stared down at it, wondering what should follow. "It's—well . . . oh, it's *Gay!*" she said brightly, as if she had been thinking of something else. "Carol Gay—spelled with one R in the Carol."

"Your address?"

"Um-well, we're moving," she improvised hastily, "so I guess you'd better reach me at Corridon's—the modeling agency, you know." No one would know her there but he could try.

"Equity card?"

"What?"

"Do you have an Equity card?" he asked patiently.

"Mercy, no. I haven't even had a part, yet." Parri had to grin at that one. "Oh, I know," she said. "You can't get an Equity card until you have a job, and you can't get a job until you have an Equity card. I've never been able to get either one."

"It could be arranged." He looked up from his careful scribbling to ask, "How old are you?"

"Fourteen." Parri decided to be honest.

"Go to school?"

"To the Theater Children's School," she said promptly, remembering a little boy in one of her mother's plays.

"Parents?"

"Oh, sure." She was playing a different part now,

and decided to be a little tough, like April. "Two," she said pertly, "the usual number," and watched him write that down.

They had nothing more to say to each other. He had no authority to offer her the part even though he wanted to, and she couldn't accept it. Their incredible contact had ended, so she became Parri MacDonald again, a girl who had been reared to be polite, and said, "Thank you for bothering with me." But it seemed he wasn't through.

"We'd like to talk to your parents," he said. "You're a minor, you know, so we'd have to talk with them before we could make a decision and offer you a contract." A door opened and closed, then footsteps sounded on the dusty floor near the dressing room; and, shading his eyes to see beyond the lighted circle, he went on, "If you'll give me your address we'll get in touch with them."

"I can't." Those footsteps just might be her father's. They didn't sound like his, and it seemed impossible that he could have traced her here, but Parri was in a fever of impatience to pass whoever was out there in the gloom. "I'll have to go," she said. "I'm late for an appointment. It was very kind of you to . . ." And then a man came out on the stage, and she had to whirl around and stand with her back to him.

She knew him. It was Mr. Moorehouse, a producer like her father, and a long-time friend of her parents.

"Hi, Jim," he said, not noticing her at all, but going straight to the table where the pile of scripts and typewritten papers lay. "Do you have that diagram for lighting handy?"

"It's right here, sir."

The young man hurried over to the table, and Parri thought it a most opportune moment to retrieve her coat and purse, and flee. The only way she could reach them was to walk backward until she was past the table, then make a sudden whirl and grab. And she was halfway into her coat and reaching for her purse when the man called Jim said, "I'd like you to meet this young lady, Mr. Moorehouse. She's been reading Maggie for me, and I was just taking down some information about her. Miss Gay?"

"Uhhh!" Parri straightened up with her purse clutched against her and gave one horrified glance at the two men, then turned and went streaking off into the dark. Catastrophe had almost overtaken her. It had even nipped at her heels, but she was safe. The heavy outside door swung shut behind her, and she stood in the alley and shook.

"Oh, I never should have done it, I never should have done it," she kept groaning, all the way back to Broadway and all along the blocks to the office building where a frantic father was sure to be housed. "*Whatever* made me do such a thing?" she asked nobody in particular, but amusing the people she passed. "No wonder Daddy was afraid to leave me. No wonder Mums knew I needed a little-girl kind of coat. I'm not to be trusted. Oh, *dear!*"

She was almost hysterical by the time she reached the offices of MacDonald Productions, Incorporated, and she stumbled out of the elevator at the eighteenth floor without once having thought of the part she most surely could have had. Only one sad fact filled her mind: it could be two o'clock, or three, or even later, and she wasn't in the coat she had been sent to buy.

Her hand hovered over the doorknob, afraid to touch it, and she pressed her ear against the heavy mahogany door, not knowing what she expected to hear. Police calls probably, telephones ringing, her father's voice begging detectives to go out and *search!*

But all was quiet. There was even the distant clack of a typewriter tapping, so she gathered enough courage to open the door a little way and slide through.

"Why, Miss Parri," the girl at the switchboard in the outer lobby looked up to say. "Everybody's been wondering where you were. Your mother telephoned about one o'clock and asked you to call her back, and she's been calling regularly ever since. Your father was delayed and just came in. He's calling your mother now."

"Thank you. I'm a little late myself," Parri answered, so weak with relief that she went staggering down the long corridor. She wasn't in the clear yet, she knew, but she was better off than she had hoped to be. She was over two hours late, but her father hadn't known it until a few minutes ago.

"Hello, Daddy," she said, standing in the doorway of his walnut-paneled office. "I've had my lunch."

"Good grief, Pen, here she is!" Her father at the telephone looked up, then said into the mouthpiece, "She says she's eaten, and she's got on the coat. I'll bring her right home. She's all right, darling, so don't cry. Yes, she's dressed up like Mrs. Astor's plush horse. Yes, we'll start right away, dear. I know. I know, Pen. Try to stop crying, honey, we're coming." Then he laid the receiver back into its cradle and sat looking across his desk. "Well?" he said.

"I met a girl named April Showers in a drugstore," Parri answered, wishing she could sit down and save her legs. "We had lunch together and she was a lovely girl. I liked her. And . . ." Something told Parri to skip over her post-luncheon activities, for now at least. Her father had enough to be angry about. "And I bought the wrong coat," she said. "I know I did everything wrong, Daddy, but it all seemed so sort of—sort of accidental."

"Some day!" Josh sat staring at her, still so upset that he couldn't have told if the coat she wore was red, green, or pale blue. Then he gave a deep sigh and flipped the switch of a small box on his desk. "Have my car brought over, Marie," he said. And after that he and Parri just looked at each other.

Josh didn't trust himself to speak. He blamed himself for having let go of Parri, for not being here at one o'clock, for not having left word where he could be reached. But, aside from bolstering Penny, what could he have done? His office manager had called all the hospitals, his secretary had spent the afternoon running up and down the block. Coming back on time to take Parri to lunch wouldn't have helped. Parri wasn't here.

She was old enough to be trusted to do what she had been told, he thought angrily. Or was she? His eyes softened a little as he looked at the drooping figure that had moved inside just far enough to close the door. It looked ridiculous in that coat, and any girl old enough to be out on her own would have had the good sense to recognize it. Parri just wasn't ready to make proper decisions. Then he remembered Penny at home crying, and his eyes grew stern again. "We'll wait downstairs," he said, and got up to fill his briefcase.

Parri's fiery red coat wasn't mentioned during the long drive home. Neither was her luncheon with a strange girl nor the lost two hours, because they didn't talk at all. Josh drove and Parri sat beside him, wishing he would speak to her. He wished he could. He wished he could think of something to say. Penny would, he knew. She would be as voluble as he was silent, and in almost every other sentence she would threaten to murder Parri. She would ask questions, then cry; Parri would answer and cry, and they'd begin to get somewhere. He could only concentrate on his driving; and it was a relief to them both when he pulled into their driveway and parked beside their long, rambling white house. The fireworks were about to begin.

Penny came rushing out, still showing the traces of recent tears. "Parrish MacDonald," she cried, just as Josh had expected, "I could *murder* you! I could simply murder you in cold blood!" And then she collided with Joshu and his Saint Bernard and wailed, "Now, where did *you* come from? Blitz, stop barking! Joshu, make him move so I can see what Parri looks like. *Oh, my heavens!*"

Parri had come reluctantly out of the bucket seat, and Josh thought Penny was going to sit right down in the driveway. She sagged, but she couldn't fall because a dog as big as a pony was pressed against her. She only closed her eyes and said feebly, "Joshu, go away. Please go somewhere and take Blitz with you."

"And not watch Parri get murdered? Oh gosh, Ma." Joshu, a small duplicate of his father, hitched up his jeans and looked pityingly at Parri from under a drooping bang of black hair. "She's a sight," he volunteered, privately thinking the coat would bug all her friends. But Penny gave him a push.

"Go on," she said more calmly, having recovered from her initial shock. Then, without another word, she turned around and went back into the house.

"We'd better follow her," Josh said, and it surprised him to find that he had taken his daughter's cold trembling hand in his. "I'm not on your side, remember," he went on, "so don't get any ideas. It's just that you're so much younger than we are. Hop along in there."

The way led past the kitchen, where Minna, the cook, and her handy-man husband looked sadly out. John tried to smile encouragement and Minna stopped wiping her eyes on her apron, but Parri was looking down at the carpet.

They found Penny in the long, low-ceilinged living room, sitting on a green-upholstered sofa. Her brown curls were rumpled, and her big brown eyes, so like Parri's, were filled with stunned disbelief. She hadn't really believed Parri could have chosen anything so wrong for her. Pricewise, yes, but not . . . "I don't know what to say," she groaned; and that, for Penny Parrish MacDonald, was more than an admission of defeat. Then she held out her hand and said, "Give me the coat."

Parri was glad to slide out of the garment that had been so beautiful just a few hours before. She hated it now; and she watched her mother lay it across her lap, smooth down the rumpled fur, even run her finger along the streak of mustard above the wide cuff. "I'm sorry," she said, and Penny looked up.

"That won't help us much," she answered coldly. And then she asked, "Did you know how much this coat cost when you bought it?" Parri's head shook in denial, so she went on, "Then I'll tell you. It cost seven hundred and fifty dollars. Seven hundred and fifty dollars."

"Oh, Mums, take it back!" Parri's mouth was a large round O that filled with an inrush of air and choked her. "Oh, oh, oh," she gasped, and threw herself at her mother's feet.

But Penny only moved the coat away from Parri's burrowing face and laid it over the arm of the sofa. "I can't. You wore it out of the store," she said. "Now *I'll* have to wear it this winter. I wanted a black coat, but I'll have to wear a red one. I'll have to have it lengthened, some way, and wear it."

"You always look good in red, Pen," Josh said,

from over by the fireplace, where he was poking simmering logs into flame. "You had a red coat when I first met you, remember?" he added, trying to offer her some comfort. "I always liked you in it."

"But it wasn't up to my *knees!* And it wasn't too tight in the shoulders, and it didn't cost seven hundred and fifty dollars. It cost thirty-nine ninety-five, on sale." Penny sighed and closed her eyes. "I think you'd better go up to your room, Parri," she said, "before I forget how much I love you and decide to tear you limb from limb and chop you up in little pieces. Go on."

"But, Mummie. . . ."

"Go on, Parri. I have to sit here and think. I've done nothing else since Miss Heatheridge told me what you'd done, and since you went off on your own. I want to *try* to handle this thing calmly, so I need your father's advice. We'll call you when we're ready to talk to you."

Parri got up slowly. The telephone was ringing in the library, and to ease her exit she asked, "Shall I answer it?"

"No, I'll get it." Josh passed her at the foot of the hall stairway. He would have liked to give her desolate shoulders a pat, but he only watched her drag herself up the stairway, then went on to stop the telephone's insistent ringing.

Penny sat staring into the fire, wondering how her mother would have handled such a situation had one of her children stepped out of line and bought something without first asking the price. But none of them would have thought of doing it on an army officer's salary. Every dollar counted in those days, so there was no comparison between Penny Parrish, daughter of a major with no outside income, and Parrish MacDonald, who thought all her mother and father had to do to get money was walk into a theater's box office and take what they wanted. She was considering putting on the blasted coat and driving over to her parents for advice when Josh came back.

"Well, are you ready for act two of this gosh-awful day?" he asked, sitting down beside her. "There's more to come, so you'd better be strong."

"I can take it." Penny turned to face him, sure they had suddenly gone bankrupt. The new play had probably closed and all their investments had failed. In a flash of imagination she saw herself down on her knees before Miss Heatheridge, holding up the coat and imploring her to take it back. "What else has happened?" she asked in little more than a whisper.

"That was Lew Moorehouse on the phone. It seems we now have another actress in the family."

They were solvent! They could pay for the coat! In her relief, Penny said in a daze, "Oh, thank goodness."

"Thank goodness what?"

"That we haven't gone broke. You scared me for a minute. What did Lew mean by saying we have another actress? We haven't."

"We have Parri."

"*Parri?*"

They stared at each other until Penny asked again, wonderingly, "Why should Lew want Parri?"

"He doesn't." Josh pulled her over against him as he said, "You'd better rest against my shoulder, so if you faint you'll fall on me. Our daughter tried out for a part in Lew's show this afternoon. Miss Carol Gay she was."

"Oh, Josh, you're teasing!" Penny pushed herself up to look at him, but one glance into his steady eyes told her he wasn't. "Go on, tell me," she said, dropping back against him again.

"All right, here goes." He made the story as brief as he could by relating, "It seems that Lew had his assistant director casting bit parts. He had tried out several duds for an ingenue's little scene and was getting discouraged when in tripped Miss Carol Gay in a red coat."

"Parri?"

"Parri. And she was good."

"She'd better have been," Penny said to his great surprise. "I'd murder her if she'd flopped. But go on. How did he know it was our Parri?"

"She got all mixed up about her name. She

41

was evasive with the director about her parents and hadn't an Equity card or a home address. And about the time the guy had settled for him to reach her through some modeling agency, Lew walked in. He only got a quick look at her, and at first he thought it was you—the fancy grown-up coat, I suppose—and by the time he saw it wasn't, she was streaking out of there. It took him a couple of hours to put two and two together, and another one to make up his mind to call out here and ask what the joke was."

"Oh, mercy. What did you tell him?"

"The truth. I told him Parri had been on a binge all day, but that it won't happen again because I'll probably whale her within an inch of her life and then you'll murder her."

"Oh, Josh, this is serious."

"Darn serious."

Penny sat up again and ran her fingers through her hair. "Why should Parri want to try out for a play without telling us?" she asked, distressed. "Has she been secretly plotting it, or was it just one of those things that happen accidentally?"

"That's what she told me. She said it was all unplanned, but we'll have to grill her."

"She shouldn't have done it, Josh."

"That I know."

"So I suppose we'll have to hold a court-martial." Penny jumped up and began pacing about the room. "Oh, merciful heavens!" she cried. "I thought buying the coat was enough, and now comes this! But we'll give her a fair trial, like the one I had when I got lost from David and Carrol and went off with Miss Ware. We'll give her every chance to explain. Oh, dear."

She began to cry, and Josh got up to put his arms around her. He caught her between a small chair and a massive carved chest, and they stood wedged in, with Penny's face buried in his shoulder. "I don't want her not to be happy living the way she is," Penny sobbed. "She's just a little girl, and I don't want her not to like living with us and to want to go off and be an actress."

"We don't know that she does, darling," Josh comforted, knowing a little more about Parri's day than Penny did. "It was probably just something she got into and was having fun with. Like a game." And then he told her about April Showers. "You see, darling, we'll have to hear Parri's side of the story before we condemn her. We know about the coat, but we aren't very clear about this other business."

"Yes."

Penny dried her eyes and raised her head. Her mother and father had always held fair hearings for their children. Each child had stated his or her side, and their parents had stated theirs. It had been as impartial as an army trial, and a verdict had always been reached, with proper punishment for the culprit. "Should we call Mums

43

and Dad over?" she asked, going over to sit wearily down again.

"No, not yet."

Josh would have liked to, because, as an orphan, he loved his parents-in-law. He felt closer to them than he did to the uncle who had halfheartedly tried to rear him, and he truly believed that their unbiased minds would be better in this crisis than his and Penny's. His was filled with pity for his daughter, and Penny's was too changeable to be any good at all. They both loved Parri and they both loved the theater. So how, he asked himself, could you judge a kid for wanting something that you yourself couldn't live without?

"I guess it's our job, Pen," he said. "Are you calm enough to call her down now?" And just then the front door opened.

CHAPTER 3

"WE'RE SORRY WE'RE LATE, DEARS," Mrs. Parrish called from the hall, looking through the archway at Penny, sitting like a statue on the sofa, and at Josh, frozen before the chest. "Carrol and David were late picking us up," she explained. "David had a meeting of some kind and . . ." She broke off to move farther inside so others could come in behind her: her husband, her son and daughter-in-law, young Lang, and lastly Davy, who shoved his brother aside so he could close the door. "Mercy, Penny," she said, giving Colonel Parrish her purse to hold so she could take off her coat, "don't look so stricken. We aren't *that* late!"

"That late—for what?" Penny asked, coming to life but looking bewildered.

"Why, for dinner, child." Colonel Parrish moved to the front of the group and said, "Are we all out of our minds to think you invited us this morning?"

"I did? Oh, my goodness." Penny clasped her head in her hands and murmured in a dazed way, "Why, so I did. It was just about noon," she remembered aloud, "and I had just hung up from hearing Susan say that she and Bobby couldn't come because he has to work late, when the phone rang. After that, everything became so awful . . . Oh, dear!" she cried. "I even forgot to tell Minna. We haven't enough to eat."

"What became so awful, Pen?" David asked, tossing all the coats he held on a chair. "Good Lord, what happened that was awful enough to make you forget you were giving a family party?"

"Parri," Josh said, thinking they looked like a bunch of bewildered sheep crowded in a pen, so releasing them by saying, "Come on in. Miss Parri did a repeat on Penny's Big Day in New York of twenty years ago. Only she spent seven hundred and fifty dollars and got herself a part in a play."

"She didn't!"

Three said the words simultaneously, and the rest stared at him the way Penny was staring at them. Then they flooded into the living room and stood in front of the sofa.

"What happened, Penny?" the lovely blond Carrol asked, moving a red coat aside so she could sit down. "How on earth could Parri go out and spend seven hundred and fifty dollars?"

"Buying that." Penny pointed to the coat, and as Carrol pulled it across her knees, she said, "That's what I'll have to wear this winter." And she began to cry again.

"Darling!" Mrs. Parrish bent over her, the two brown heads close together. Mrs. Parrish's had gray threads in it and little gray wings, but she and Penny looked much alike. Just as David and his older son resembled Colonel Parrish in a broad-shouldered blond way, although Colonel Parrish's hair was quite white now and glasses hid his kind blue eyes. "Crying isn't like you, dear," Mrs. Parrish said. "Not over a *coat*. It might make you justly angry, or even furious, but I can't see why it would block out everything else."

"It's only the beginning," Penny managed to say, wiping her eyes. "Disobeying me and buying such an expensive coat was bad enough, but—oh, dear, you tell them, Josh."

"Well . . ." Josh wondered where to begin. They were all looking at him: David in front of the mantel, one foot hooked over the brass fender; Colonel Parrish still holding his wife's purse as if it were a package; Davy with his hands thrust deep in his pockets, and scowling uncomfortably; and young Lang, his bright dark eyes shining in anticipation. "I can only give you as much as we know ourselves," he began. "We haven't brought Parri down yet, to fill us in on the details of what we just learned, but here it is." And he proceeded to give them an account of Parri's day from the minute he had left her in New York.

"That about does it," he said at the end. "She bought the coat you see here, and she disappeared for almost three hours and scared Penny frantic. She met a girl she calls April Showers, and how she managed to land backstage at the Gantry—well, your guess is as good as mine. Shall we call her down and get the full story?"

"Gosh, yes." Lang thought the briefing had been thorough enough and was eager to know how Parri, a cousin who had never interested him much, had turned out to be such a whizz. He knew some cute girls who were fourteen to his sixteen, but Parri had left him cold. "She sure is nutty," he said. "Let's bring her down."

But Davy frowned at him. "This isn't any of our business," he pointed out. "We all got here by accident, so maybe you and I ought to leave. Parri's in enough trouble without having us listening in. I'd better go find Carli, Mom," he suggested, turning to his mother, "and take her home with us. Want us to take Joshu, too?"

"Wait a minute." Carrol tried to pull herself back to reality. There was still dinner to be eaten somewhere. She knew from experience that this hearing would last for some time, with the culprit finally deciding what her punishment should be. Unexpected guests never bothered her staff of servants at Gladstone, so she said, "Lang can go out to the barn to find Joshu and Carli. I want you to call Perkins and tell him . . ."

"We only have a stupid little meat loaf," Penny interrupted tremulously, also conscious of all the people who had arrived to be fed. "Perhaps the boys could find a market open somewhere."

"Silly," Carrol said, "we've loads of stuff at home." And, knowing Penny and her quick reactions, she scolded, "I've told you and *told* you to buy a big freezer."

"I know it." Penny's spirits bounced up as Carrol had expected they would, and she promised, "I will, Monday. Josh tells me the same thing, and I will."

"I'll personally see that you do. Davy?"

But Davy had come over to her. "I'll call home," he said, putting his arm around his grandmother, who was his special pal, and standing beside her, "but I'd like to say something first. I know Parri," he went on. "She's an awful lot like you, Aunt Penny. She's full of zing and imagination, and she's going to amount to something someday. I don't want to see her lose her fire." And then he looked at his grandfather, his father, and his Uncle Josh before he said carefully, "Don't get me wrong. I think these courts-martial are good. I was only four when I had my first one, and it gave me something to think about."

"Oh, Davy, you weren't!" his mother cried, startled. "You were always so *good!*"

"Don't you believe it." Davy grinned at her, and went on, "I shaved Lang's head with Dad's safety razor. Of course, Lang was only a baby and didn't have much hair to lose, but he cried like everything. You did too, Mom, and you called up Grandma and Grandpa to come over. The calm way you all handled everything sure made a Christian out of me. I really learned that Lang's dumb little head was just as tender as mine was. But even more, it darn near killed me to drop my allowance into his piggy bank every week. It was a long, drawn-out affair," he explained ruefully, "because I only got ten cents."

"I remember now," Penny said, nodding. "But you only had a dollar and a quarter to pay back. Parri has far more."

"She's got a whole day and seven hundred and fifty bucks," he put in. "I don't know which is going to cost her more, your misery all day or the coat, but she's got a whale of a debt to pay—somehow."

"I know that, Davy, but perhaps we can work out something about the coat if I wear it. It's her disobedience that I'm worried about." Penny looked helplessly at Josh, and he went around the back of the sofa to lay his hand on her shoulder.

"Parents know they're asking for suffering when they want children, honey," he said, squeezing gently. "We wanted Parri; and she's been healthy and fairly easy to manage up to now. A little stubborn and silly at times maybe, but nothing much to complain about."

"I know that." She reached up for his hand and sighed. "But I was so terribly worried about her," she moaned. "I was so terribly, terribly frightened."

"So were we," her mother reminded, "when you were lost from us until almost twelve o'clock one night."

"But that was different," Penny protested. "I telephoned and thought you'd get the message." Then she realized that telephoning without making sure she had the right number was just as bad as not telephoning at all. "You're right," she said, nodding, "I was just as careless as Parri. I hope I can remember that."

She watched Lang head reluctantly for the hall, and called after him, "Thanks, dear, for taking Joshu out of our way. It will be a big help."

Then she looked up at Davy. "I wish you'd go upstairs and get Parri for us," she said. "It doesn't seem fair for her to come down into this cold, and she admires you so much and thinks everything you do and say is wonderful. Am I right, Josh?" she tilted her head back to ask.

"On the beam," he agreed. "Davy is to Parri what David has always been to you."

"And don't forget me," Lang called from the hall where he had stopped to listen. "I'm her pain-in-the-neck, like Uncle Bobby was. Okay. I know when I'm not wanted."

Davy walked slowly up the stairway. He felt sorry for Parri, and yet he knew she deserved whatever was about to descend upon her. It was a simple case of crime and punishment, he thought sensibly, but he felt like the bailiff sent to bring the prisoner in.

"Hi," he said, finding her sitting by the window in her room, eyes cast down, hands clasped together, feet side by side, and looking like a martyr. "I suppose you know the whole group's here," he said.

"Yes." She swallowed and sighed.

"We didn't mean to be, but your mother invited us all to dinner and then forgot about it. But that isn't the point. The point is," he said, turning on a lamp, "you're in more trouble now than you were with the coat. Some guy called up and told your dad about your trying out for a part in the play."

"Oh, mercy!" She looked up at him then, and the tears spilled over. "What—what shall I do?" she asked haltingly.

"Just go down and tell them how it happened," he answered. "They're ready to listen to your story. And Parri," he said, pulling her to her feet and holding her hands, "wandering around town with a strange girl and frightening your mother out of her wits is bad enough, but buying that coat is worse. Gosh! That's what you've got to be sorry for. Are you?"

"Yes." Parri's whole face proved the honesty of her one little word, and she added, "I know that it was what started the day going wrong. I wouldn't ever do such a thing again, Davy. I wouldn't."

"And how about going to the theater and reading the part?" Davy tried to look stern, but found a grin twitching at his lips. "I think they're kind of proud of you for doing well. The whole family is proud of us kids if we make a go of something," he said quickly, when she began to look a little too pleased. "It was wrong for you to do it, but they aren't quite as mad as if you'd tried and failed. You did one thing right, at least."

"Thank you, Davy." She was in no position to

rejoice at even the briefest praise, so she said submissively, "I guess I'll have to take my punishment, whatever it is."

"How are you going to pay?"

He had her headed into the hall, and they stopped at the top of the stairway while he reminded, "You've got a seven-hundred-and-fifty-dollar debt. Just keep that in mind if you think you're going to get off easy."

"Oh me." Parri's foot faltered as it reached for a step, and she would have sat down had he not grasped her and propped her up.

"I'll work it out with you later," he said, realizing that the babble of conversation below had ceased and sure that every head was turned toward the lower hall, watching for the accused to appear. "You go in and present your case, and I'll wait around somewhere. Later on I'll show you how you can make good."

"Okay."

Parri's way to present her case was to fling herself full length on the carpet before her mother and father. She managed to clutch her mother's knees as she went down, but whatever she said was lost in sobs. And she kept weeping, "I'm sorry, I'm sorry, I'm sorry," until Penny forcibly dragged her up and shoved her in beside Carrol.

"Oh, stop it, Parri," she finally ordered in desperation, close to tears herself. "You're not being killed. You're not even getting what you deserve. Now, sit up and answer some questions. What made you do what you did today?"

"I don't know." Parri dried her tears on the handkerchief her father passed down to her and carefully considered a true answer as she had been taught to do. "I felt grown up, I guess," she finally said. "I bought that awful coat because I didn't want to go on being a baby. I didn't want to look ten years old, like Joshu. I wanted to be—sophisticated. And after I put on the coat, I *was*. I wasn't me any more. I was more like April," she said to the room in general. "Only—well . . . it's hard to explain. I wasn't *exactly* like April. I know I was still Parri MacDonald, but I didn't feel like her. So . . ." she gave her head a quick shake to clear it, and said, ". . . I pretended to be Carol Gay. Davy says you've heard about Carol Gay," she stated.

"Yes, we have." It was her father who answered, and he leaned over the back of the sofa to ask, "What had you planned to do if we shouldn't ever hear about her?"

"Nothing." Parri shook her head again, but more slowly.

"Would you have let a busy young director waste his valuable time hunting for a girl who doesn't exist?" Josh asked. "It doesn't sound exactly honorable to me."

"I guess it isn't." Parri felt like an untrained hurdler in a college track meet, faced with obstacles he can't possibly clear, as she said, "If anybody can tell me something to do to fix things, I'll do it."

"How about this?" Unexpectedly, it was Colonel Parrish who spoke up. "How about writing the director a note of apology?" he suggested.

"I'll do it right away," Parri answered gratefully, and she would have jumped up had not Penny held her down.

"Tonight will do," Penny said. And she explained carefully, "We're grateful that you did at least one thing right today. You did read the part well. If you hadn't we couldn't be as calm as we are. But that doesn't excuse everything else that went before it. Granted that you don't like being Parrish MacDonald . . ."

"But I *do!*" Parri protested. "I mean I did, until I got so New Yorkish and grown up."

"When you thought you could become someone more important," Penny went on. "It's understandable. But you didn't need to spend seven hundred and fifty dollars to prove it to yourself."

"I didn't know I was."

"Coats have price tags."

"Not where I was." Parri was on firm ground there. "That store wouldn't be caught dead letting a customer see a price tag," she declared.

"Clerks whisper the price. Miss Heatheridge just didn't whisper to me, that's all."

"You didn't ask her to. Listen, Parri." Penny considered thoughtfully before she summed up, "You didn't buy the coat you were supposed to buy; you didn't take a taxi to Daddy's office as you were supposed to do; you . . ."

"He wasn't there," Parri interrupted in her own defense.

"But you didn't know it. You proceeded on your own merry way. Nobody can disobey orders and get by, Parri." Penny sighed and repeated. "Nobody. It can't be done. We all agree to that."

"I do too." Parri looked soberly at everyone, then tipped her head back so she could see her father behind her. "I did everything wrong," she said. "I knew it when I was doing it, but I went right on. Now, how can I fix it?"

"What do you mean, 'fix it'?" Josh asked, while the others watched and waited.

"Why, pay for the coat," Parri answered promptly. "And make up to Mums for all the worry I caused her, and to you for upsetting your office."

"It's a tall order," Josh said into the silence that followed her words. "We have to go over to Gladstone to dinner because your mother forgot she had invited the family here, but I don't think you should go with us. I think it's better for you to ask Minna to give you some supper so you can be by yourself and really plan what you're going to do."

"All right, Daddy."

Parri was thankful not to be going to Gladstone with the others, but was at a loss to know where or how to begin her planning. She supposed she should get a scratch pad and a pencil and write down some resolutions. But what? What more was there to write than she had already said? Then Davy unexpectedly came to her rescue by walking in from somewhere and saying, "I'll stick around and give her some advice. I haven't anything special planned."

"Then court is adjourned." Colonel Parrish's voice boomed out as it always had at the end of a session, and he was the first to reach Parri. "The accused sets her own sentence, as usual," he said, pulling her up and putting his arm around her. "Does that seem fair to you, Parri?"

"Oh yes, Grandpa." Parri felt her mother's kiss on her cheek and her father's hand stroking the top of her head. "I'd rather be little and get a spanking," she said, "but I can't. And, anyway, this is something too big for just a spanking. I'll —I'll work out something that will punish me."

There were more kisses, mixed with compassion and pride, from her grandmother and her aunt, more kindly pats from her uncle; then she watched her mother put on the too-small coat, and they all went away, leaving her alone with Davy.

"Oh me," she said, when he sat down and took a little notebook and ball-point pen from his pocket. "Shall we eat first," she suggested, "and think afterward? I'm kind of hungry."

But he only asked, "How much money have you?"

"Huh?" She sat down too, right where she had been, and felt suddenly cold. She had three dollars and forty-two cents.

"Bonds, savings account, that sort of thing," he persisted. "You have *something*, don't you?"

"Yes, I guess so."

Saving money, up to now, had meant very little to Parri. She had dutifully thanked her grandparents for the twenty-five-dollar savings bond they gave her on each birthday and at Christmas, but had never asked what became of them. Somewhere in the clutter of her desk was a little brown book that would tell her what birthday checks her mother had deposited in the bank for her, but the book had almost no entries. She had cashed most of the checks to buy something she had wanted very much at the time. "Well, let me see," she began desperately. "If Grandma and Grandpa started giving me bonds when I was just a baby, that ought to be . . ." But Davy interrupted her.

"Did they?" he asked.

"I don't know."

She looked across at him, hoping that, by some miracle, she would have hundreds and hundreds of beautiful dollars in a safety box somewhere, but he only got up and went off to the telephone.

"They started when you were five," he said, coming back and sitting down again to figure. "The same as they did for Lang and me. That makes eight years of bonds, plus the one you got a couple of weeks ago."

"Oh, good!" Relief washed over Parri's heart like a tidal wave. All those little pieces of paper that she hadn't wanted or ever thought about again were snugly tucked away to save her. Those dear, darling little pieces of paper. "I'm rich!" she cried. "Oh, thank goodness, I'm rich!"

But Davy was adding. "Sixteen twenty-five-dollar bonds and the last one you got make four hundred and twenty-five dollars. That leaves you with three hundred and twenty-five still to pay. What else have you got?"

"Nothing much," she mumbled, so deflated he could barely hear her. For all Davy's help she wasn't much better off; and, checking amounts on her fingers, she said, "I saved two dollars out of Uncle Bobby's five-dollar birthday checks—twice; and ten dollars from your mother's check for this birthday; and three, and a dollar, and . . . well," she ended, after much agony of silent counting, "I guess I have thirty-five dollars in my savings account."

"Not bad." Davy looked cheerful while he added his dinky column again, then he looked up to ask, "What allowance do you get?"

"A dollar and a half a week," she answered without hesitation, sure of the pitiful answer to that question. "But fifty cents of it has to go for school activities, you see."

"Okay." Davy, intent on more black figures, looked up with a grin. "That's swell," he said, even though he knew he was about to deliver her a knockout blow. "Counting the bonds from Grandma and Grandpa for two more birthdays and Christmases, and all your allowance, you'll have the debt paid off in a little less than two years. That's pretty good, isn't it?"

"Oh, oh, *ohhh*," Parri wept. "I can't bear it!"

"You bore being a big shot today just fine," he reminded. "You lived big today."

"But I—oh *deeear!*" Parri wiped her eyes on a green brocade pillow and wailed, "I didn't mean to. Maybe I can sell all my—my possessions."

"What, for instance?"

Davy watched her suffer. Her punishment had been left to her, and it had been fairly easy up to now. He had stayed behind for the simple purpose of showing her that her gay misadventure would be costly. He knew from experience how hard it was to pay back a debt. Even at four he had known and decided to pay for the haircut. Now, at eighteen, he was paying for his case of infantile paralysis that hadn't been his fault. His young body had had a weakness somewhere, so he was paying.

"Listen, Parri," he said calmly, "if you're thinking of selling any stuff your folks gave you, you might as well forget it. They'd only have to buy you more. Personal possessions—okay. What have you got that you bought and paid for yourself?"

Parri tried to think. What did she have that was salable and bought with gift money? "My charm bracelet," she decided at last. "A girl at school offered me two dollars for it."

"Okay. What else?"

"My archery set. It cost eighteen dollars, and Joshu wouldn't put out so much for just a bow and some arrows. Maybe he'll give me ten, though. He said he would, once."

"One archery set duly entered. Anything more?" Davy asked, nodding at Minna, who stood in the hall to remind them that the meat loaf, small as it had been, was rapidly shrinking to a cinder.

"I'll have to think." Parri got up and followed him to the dining room, obedient but bowed under a financial weight that seemed heavier on her shoulders than the budgets grown people are supposed to carry.

"If you can dig up fifty bucks more," Davy encouraged her, eating meat loaf and vegetables as if they were the only important things in life, "you'll be in the clear in a year." And then, feeling that she had had enough for one session, he asked chattily, "Did you know Bitsy Jordon gets home next week?"

"Yes."

Parri was well aware of Bitsy's return from visiting a married sister in England. All the Jordons had been either saying it or writing it in letters, and there were a great number of them to pass the word along. One of them had become her uncle, because Captain Peter Jordon had married her aunt Tippy, and one had become her aunt when Susan married her Uncle Bobby. Three other daughters had married and moved away, but Neal was a first classman in West Point, and Vance was a plebe, exactly what Davy longed to be.

Poor Davy, she thought, looking across the table at him. He tried so hard never to limp when he was tired, and he did like Bitsy so much. He was so kind. Here he sat, helping her out of a muddle, when he might have been home practicing with after-shave lotion and putting goo on his hair, or whatever boys did when the girl of their dreams came home. Her heart became suddenly so filled with love and pity that she stopped trying to conjure up valuables to sell and said in a most interested way, "Bitsy's a charming girl. I think it's nice that you're in love with her."

"I'm not in love, you dope!" Davy slapped down his fork and glared at her. "Who told you that?" he demanded.

"Why, no one. It just sticks out all over you." With sudden misgiving she wondered if she should back up a little and assure him that it was just his good-natured interest in everybody that stuck out. What if he should get mad and withdraw his support? He couldn't take back the sound financial advice he had already given her, but he might not be receptive to future confidences, or care how discouraged she got with poverty. "I mean," she said, pretending she hadn't noticed his glare, "you're always so kind and loving, Davy. You take time to help me, and you were always picking Bitsy up at school last spring and driving her to town to buy clothes for her trip, and you sat right in the front row at her graduation, and invited her to yours at the Academy, and . . ."

"Oh, dry up." For a moment it looked as if Davy might push back from the table and go off to finish his dinner at home; then he went on eating. "You're a dope," he said, when Parri had begun to think their silence might last forever. And with great good nature and an air of conspiracy, he winked at her.

CHAPTER 4

Days dragged by for Parri. She had no dimes to put in the vending machine at school for chocolate bars and caramels; she couldn't afford to go to the village with the boys who lived down the road because they expected her to pay for what she ate or drank in the drugstore. It didn't help much that her parents had watched her shove her first dollar bill into a yellow pig that would have been rib-thin had it not been made of china, and told her how proud they were of her. Parri only squeezed back the tears and wondered how she could ever wait for a hundred and four Mondays to pass; or, even worse, seven hundred and thirty dull, empty days. She would have nothing to do but eat free meals and breathe free air.

Joshu had refused to buy her bow and arrows; the girl at school was still willing to take the charm bracelet, but the most she could pay was a dollar, and she wouldn't have that until the first of the month when her check from home came. That was the trouble with a girls' school, Parri reflected miserably: nobody had any money. And what little they did have they hung onto. Nothing to sell, nothing to do.

And, added to everything else, there was the problem of April. April would be watching the mails at Corridon's, waiting for an invitation from a girl who didn't bother to keep a promise. Parri didn't think it fair for her punishment to affect April. And on the morning when she had pushed her second dollar bill into the greedy pig, with no one looking on to commend her, she wandered down to the kitchen where Minna was washing dishes and Joshu was frying an egg.

"Where's Mums?" she asked, cross because her feeding-the-pig ceremony had been a miserable affair without witnesses.

"She went to the city with your father," Minna answered; and she added pointedly, "to have *that coat* altered. It's my day off, so she said you're to go to your Grandma's after school."

"I'd rather go to Aunt Susan's," Parri answered, feeling contrary.

"Okay. She said you're just to write down where you're going."

"Or maybe I'll go to Davy's."

"You can't." Minna was large, and she had to squeeze between Parri and the stove to rescue Joshu's egg in time. "You're taking up all the room," she grumbled, putting the egg on a plate and adding several slices of bacon. "Mr. Davy's going to the doctor's, and Mrs. Parrish will be someplace I couldn't make out, with Lang, so you're to see that Carli gets off the school bus and keep her with you."

"I don't want to."

Joshu's egg looked goldenly beautiful, but Parri turned away from it and picked up one of the cereal bowls on the counter. "Carli's just a little bitty kid," she said. "I'll take her to Grandma's, and that's all I'll do for her."

She knew she sounded as grumpy as she felt, and hated herself for it; but she hated Joshu too, for not buying her archery set. She hated the way he looked, with his shirttail out and a strip of bacon hanging out of his mouth. "You're disgusting," she said to him, spooning up cereal with dainty care.

"Sure," he answered cheerily, hauling in the bacon like a plank meeting a saw. "I'm a disgusting aperture."

"Apparition," she corrected with disdain. "It means ghost, and you certainly aren't one. You're a live, horrid, nasty, little boy." And she left her unfinished breakfast and marched out.

It was while she was putting on the really good-looking camel's hair coat her mother had had Miss Heatheridge send out that she considered telephoning Davy and asking him if it would be fair to sell her doll collection to one of the toy stores in New York. The dolls had come from all over the world, and they made quite a valuable collection, like stamps or old coins, and would get her out of debt in a hurry. But Davy had abandoned her. After his one burst of kindness he had gone off about his own affairs and was never home when she called him. She didn't know it, but Davy had his own problem.

The days dragged for him too. He was waiting impatiently for Bitsy Jordon to come home, and he had learned through the family grapevine that her flight had been postponed ten days. Bitsy's father had told Susan, Susan had told Mrs. Parrish, Mrs. Parrish had passed the news on to Davy's mother, and finally it had filtered down to him, on Wednesday morning, when he had been watching across Gladstone's rolling parkland for a car to turn in at the gate.

The Jordons lived just inside the gate, in a tall white house with a gabled roof and a tower on one corner. Once it had been an imposing gatehouse for the large estate, but when the Jordons had needed a home, Gladstone Gates had been offered to them, and now the two families lived near each other, in close and pleasant companionship.

Davy, standing under a tree that let its leaves fall with sleepy carelessness, waited and watched. A car did turn in, but it was only his mother's station wagon, and it followed the long winding roadway until it stopped beside him.

"Hop in," his mother said, holding open the door. "It's no use going down to see Bitsy because she won't be home until next Saturday. I just heard." So Davy had learned that he must go on waiting.

He wasn't in love with Bitsy, as Parri had so quaintly put it. He knew that. He liked her, he trusted her, and he needed her more at this time than he needed anyone else. He had a goal to reach, and only Bisty would be able to know whether he was making progress or not. At least so he told himself.

There was nothing to do but wait, so he waited. And on Monday afternoon he went out to the stables to saddle his horse and take his daily ride.

"It's like this, Sing," he said, crossing his arms on the saddle and resting his chin on them. "I don't want to get my hopes up and try for the Point again if I haven't a chance. But I've got to make it, somehow. I've just got to. Oh, I know it's a long shot," he went on, when Singing

Star looked around, wondering why Davy didn't mount up and give the signal to leave this dull stable for the bright outdoors. "But I'm sure my leg's improving, I really am. It's a lot stronger, and it's a good inch bigger around than it was. Bitsy would know if it's filling out. She's the only one besides the doctors who saw it when it was such a mess, so she'd know if it looks better."

He sighed, gathered up his reins, then left his hand on Singing Star's neck. He had always been ashamed of his thin, weak leg that had no muscles stretching its skin. From the time he could talk, he had wanted to become an army officer, like his grandfather. He had wanted to go to West Point, as all the other Parrish men had, and had never understood why his father had resigned his commission after the war, and his Uncle Bobby after only three years. The Parrishes, for four generations, had been army men.

"I guess I feel that I'm part of the line," he told Sing, swinging into the saddle at last. "Or else we all want something we can't have. Anyway, I'm going to make one more try for what *I* want. Dad can be satisfied with turning into a farmer and Lang can take a business course and manage Mom's millions—but me? If I can pass the next physical for West Point, that's all I ask."

Davy had exercised almost to the point of exhaustion for two years. While he had been in a junior military academy, he had tried out for every sport, not caring if he made only the second team or the "scrub." He had been a pinch hitter on the baseball team, a relief relay runner on the track, reduced to head linesman for football, and substitute guard on the basketball squad. But he had kept on trying, and he had won his letter as a champion swimmer. Then, in spite of all his progress, he had failed his physical examination last spring. So this year, instead of going off to college with all his friends, he was reviewing a few subjects at Claymore Academy and working out in its heated pool and gymnasium. And he walked there and back. He walked, swam, exercised, and rode his horse every day, until sometimes at night he was too tired to crawl into bed.

"You're crazy," Lang had said last summer, when Davy was using his own outdoor pool and acrobatic equipment. "What's so important about going to the Point?"

He had walked into Davy's room unexpectedly, and from force of habit Davy had pulled down his pajama leg. He had always done that until two years ago when Bitsy Jordon had scolded him for being oversensitive. A leg was a leg, whether it matched its mate or not, she had said, when he confessed to being ashamed of his. And that was when he plunged into athletics in a serious way. Since then he always played tennis in shorts, and let anyone who cared to look see him in bathing trunks.

Bitsy was really quite a gal, he thought, letting Singing Star clop-clop across the cobbled courtyard. Not because she had big blue eyes and feathery blond curls, a pert nose, and all the right curves in all the right places; not even because she had a cute British accent that was a holdover from her childhood spent in England with Jenifer, or because she gave him a good game of tennis yet ran for her life at the sight of a tiny little field mouse in the stable. She had integrity, and she frankly admitted her faults. She would either laugh at them or be regretful and apologetic, and Davy knew she was sincere. Riding across the fields, it seemed to him that Saturday would never come.

It finally did, of course, as long-awaited days always do, and it brought Elizabeth Jordon with it. One minute—or so it seemed to her—she was far out above the Atlantic, alone in the night; the next, she was standing in her own big living room in bright morning sunshine, hugging dear Irish Ellin, who had taken care of little Jordons ever since their mother had died.

"Oh, Ellin, it's so good to be home!" she cried, tossing her coat down and dancing across the room to her father, who was looking longingly at his big easy chair. "I missed you both ever so much."

"Good—er hur-rumph—good." General Jordon always cleared his throat under any emotional strain, and once it had terrified Bitsy. Now it made her laugh.

"How's the big executive doing?" she asked, their whole drive home having been filled with her account of Jenifer and her two children. "Have you and Ellin rattled around here alone?" she pursued. "Or did Neal and Vance come home on weekends and Susan drop in every day?" She had a whole list of questions to ask, because she had stayed awake most of the night on the plane, considering her life here at home and what she should do with it. Should she go back to the funny little bookshop and work for Miss Jeffers, or would her father be enough adjusted to being alone so she could live in New York and take the course in fashion designing she wanted so much?

"It has been—hur-rumph—very pleasant," he returned, settling down and giving Ellin a sly wink. He and Ellin had enjoyed their easy, relaxed summer. Neal had been home, but rarely seen; Vance had been in plebe summer camp; and while Susan had dropped in faithfully, she always went back to her own house and left him with long, free evenings. This fall, he had almost thought himself a bachelor again. "But I missed you," he added gallantly, leaving her as undecided as she had been on the plane.

"Perhaps I'd better nip over and see Susan," she said, thinking how hard it was to be the last child to leave home. The others had simply gone. Oh, they had been apologetic and regretful, of course, but nevertheless they had passed on their responsibilities to the next in line and gone.

"A fine idea, my dear," the General answered, unaware that they were postponing a subject Bitsy was eager to introduce. "I'm sure Susan will be here later this morning, but it might be pleasant to run about a bit. Davy Parrish is looking forward to seeing you."

"He is? Good. I may pop in over there." Bitsy smiled, and said, "I may make the rounds of all the Parrishes and the MacDonalds." And then she found herself saying, "Oh, Daddy, I missed this life. It was wonderful to be with Jenifer again, but I missed belonging to such a big family."

"Sure, and it wasn't the same without ye," Ellin put in, having been a little more lonely than General Jordon, with so few to cook for and so little hanging up and putting away to do. She had missed the carefree Jordons, their confidences and problems, and it made her happy to have Bitsy offer impulsively:

"How about coming with me, Ellin? I've such a lot to tell you and Susan, and we can bring in my luggage and unpack when the boys come. Why, where are Neal and Vance?" she stopped to ask. "It's Saturday, isn't it? I thought they'd be here, too."

"'Tis the big football game in New York," Ellin informed her proudly. "The whole corps will be there and viry grand it will look, marchin' into the stadium—with me Vancy stridin' right along with the rist of them, beside Neal, no doubt, since thir both tall and in A Company."

Bitsy was disappointed in her brothers because they preferred a football game to meeting their own sister. She had expected to see them at International Airport, not her father, so she picked up her coat and, looking out at the station wagon parked in the driveway, said crossly, "I suppose I'll have to carry in my own luggage." And then she cried, "My word! I wish you'd look who's coming!"

A horseman was skirting the parked car, followed by a humped-up blob on a small black mare. The blob's face was chalk-white, and it was attached to the saddle by two gripping hands.

Davy had intended riding over to see Bitsy, just stopping by and pulling up from an easy canter; but saddling Singing Star for the occasion, he had lost his nerve. Who was he to think Bitsy would want him to arrive so soon, even before she had had time to admire Neal and Vance in their splendid cadet uniforms? Why should she want to take time out for a lame guy on a horse when she could be flanked by gray uniforms from the

United States Military Academy? She wouldn't. Nobody would. He really had no excuse to ride in that direction. And then impoverished Parri had picked her lonesome way along the graveled road behind the garage, headed for the stable.

Davy had welcomed Parri as a good omen and a timely accomplice. A riding lesson was what she needed, he had persuaded her. With no money to spend, she could fill her lonely afternoons with learning to ride a horse. She could jog along on Meg, sometimes with him, sometimes with Lang, over hill and dale, and in no time at all she could learn to go alone. The fact that she wore her new coat, pleated skirt, and socks and brogues hadn't stopped him. Parri, willy-nilly, had been boosted aboard a phlegmatic little horse that belonged to Carli and headed toward the Jordons'.

It had been a long and bouncy ride, and she hadn't seen anything but the ground and Meg's neck. Her feet had long ago become disconnected from her stirrups, and the reins were no good to hold onto. Davy had given her instruction now and then, had told her she was doing fine, but for the last few minutes he had trotted easily in the lead and not looked back. And a parked car loomed up ahead.

"Oh, stop!" Parri commanded her busy little horse, and kept right on going.

She went past the car, she almost went past Singing Star; and when Bitsy came running down her side steps and reached up to grasp Davy's hand, she got Meg's mane instead. Even when Davy quickly dismounted to straighten things out he was blocked by a solid wall of horse that had the good sense not to move. Parri's arms were hugged around its neck and most of her hung over its face.

"Oh, gosh," Davy said, shoving her back in the saddle. "This wasn't such a hot idea." A planned accidental meeting had turned into a farce, and he had nobody to blame but himself.

"Anyway, it was wonderful of you to come by," Bitsy said, trying not to laugh. "Hello, Parri."

"Hel-hel . . . oh." Parri slid to the ground any old way and caught enough breath to finish her "hello." Then she glared at David. "If you ever do anything like this to me again," she said, furious, "I'll murder you in cold blood. You said we were just going to practice riding back and forth in the driveway. *Walking*. And you *trotted* me over here. I hate you, Davy Parrish, and I don't care how you get your old horse home!"

She started to walk away, then remembered that she hadn't really spoken to Bitsy, so came back. "It's nice to have you home, Bitsy," she said. "Did you have a good time?"

"Smashing," Bitsy replied before she thought. Then she put her arm around Parri and said, hugging her, "I mean, it was super. Come in and I'll tell you about it."

77

"No thanks, not now." Something told Parri that Davy had used her as an excuse to ride over here, so she wasn't quite so mad at him. He looked nice in his polished boots and whipcord breeches, and his tan tweed coat. In fact, he looked so dressed up that she felt almost sorry for him. Poor Davy, he didn't know how good-looking he was. "I think I'll just walk back to Gladstone," she said. And she offered kindly, "I'll lead the horses back for you, Davy, so you can go in."

"Now, why should you do that?" he asked, and her pity vanished.

He was stupid. He was stubborn and stupid; so she remarked pointedly, "No reason. I just thought one good turn deserves another, that's all. Banking business and a riding lesson, you know."

"I get you." Davy grinned at her then, but he said, "I don't want to stay. Bitsy has other things to do." And he asked, easily, in the way he usually talked, "How about a date tonight, Bits? We can catch a movie, or something."

"I'd love it." Bitsy was puzzled by the two cryptic sentences that had crossed in front of her. Parri and Davy shared a secret, and she was curious. "Sure you won't stay?" she asked them both, certain that with very little prodding Parri would come out with whatever it was.

"Nope, see you at eight." Davy turned the horses around and handed Meg's reins to Parri. "We'll catch up on everything then," he called back, looping his arms across Parri's shoulders.

"You certainly weren't much of a hero," Parri said, when they were walking the long road home. "Why didn't you tell me what you wanted, so we could have driven over and not made such a spectacle of *me?* I could have cooked up some excuse for coming."

"It just hit me all of a sudden. There you were, and I thought you'd enjoy it."

"You did not." Parri turned her head and grinned knowingly at him. She felt the way her mother must have when Davy's father had been too shy to let Carrol Houghton know how much he liked her. "Oh, I was there, all right, I'm sorry to say," she retorted. "But next time, kindly brief me."

"There won't have to be a next time because Bitsy hasn't changed at all. I was afraid she might have, but I don't think she has." And he asked, "Do you?"

Parri was proud to be consulted, and she considered her answer carefully. "I don't see why she should change," she finally said, "not in four months."

"Because she's been going around with lords and viscounts, and even a duke," he reminded. "Most girls would fall in a faint if a duke asked them out."

"But you're you, Davy." Parri stopped and let Meg butt into her while she told him, "You're Davy

Parrish. There isn't anybody else like you in the whole world. Don't you know that?"

"Yeah, and it's not much to be."

"It's everything. Listen," she said, walking on again, "I messed up my life something fierce a few Saturdays ago, but I know I did it because I'm me. I act like me, and think like me, and do like me. You're you, Davy. Don't you realize you're a you that any girl would want to date?"

"I guess I can't see it."

"Well, you'd better. You're pretty wonderful," she said. "I can't explain things very well, but if you go on being the person you are inside, Bitsy and everything else you want will come your way."

"Thanks, pal." Davy gave her shoulders a little squeeze, then reached down and took Meg's reins from her. "You're unusually wise for fourteen," he said.

"I live in a wise family," she answered. "It's a little hard sometimes, and I forget to remember it, so if you see me slipping please feel free to jack me up."

"Will do."

They walked on in silence, Davy wondering if by being himself he could attain the future he wanted, and Parri wishing she could think of some way to win back the allowance she needed so badly.

CHAPTER 5

The china pig was six dollars fatter. Brilliant autumn had changed to bleak, cold November, and Parri MacDonald had put in the longest, dreariest time of her whole fourteen years. Her mother had found it even harder.

Penny, getting up from her desk in the upstairs office she and Josh shared, was sure Parri would be waiting for her somewhere. She usually was. She came straight home from school to tag along or seat herself in the car. So to find her sitting on the top step of the stairway was no surprise. She made a habit of sitting there on Saturday mornings.

"Hi, pet," Penny said, having prepared herself

for this, and dreading it. "Move over and make room for me."

Parri slid along the carpet, and Penny sat down beside her. "I want to talk to you about this punishment you set yourself," she began, leaning back against the newel post. "Both Daddy and I felt it was much too severe."

"You did?" Parri looked up wonderingly. "I thought you liked it," she said in a weak voice.

"We were proud of you, dear, but we didn't think you needed to go to such an extreme. We tried to tell you that, but you were so insistent on being honorable that we decided to let you go ahead and try it."

"Oh."

Parri recalled that fateful Sunday morning, vividly and with regret. She had come into the library where her mother and father were having their second cup of coffee and reading the New York newspapers, and had announced her plan. She had even produced a piece of paper with Davy's figures on it, but written in her own handwriting, and declared, "This is what I want to do. You let me set my own punishment, and this is what I think I should do."

Now, remembering the way her parents had looked at each other, she wished she had said honestly, "This is what Davy thinks I should do." Davy could have the credit, the whole six weeks of it, if only she hadn't bustled in and tried to be noble. But she listened to Penny saying:

"I'm wearing the coat, Parri. It's far more expensive than any I would have bought, but after some alteration it looks nice and people admire it. There's no reason why you should pay full price for a coat I can wear."

"I'd like to," Parri put in, still trying.

"That's sweet of you and I appreciate it. But listen, honey." Penny slid around and took one of Parri's limp hands in hers. "This is the way it is," she said. "The fact that you were eager to pay for your disobedience is what counts. I have the coat. I like it, I can afford it; but because I couldn't exchange it for a larger size, I had to have it altered. Why don't you simply pay for the alterations?"

"Were they very expensive?" Parri asked, wondering how long her pig would have to go on eating.

"Three of your bonds and what you've already saved," Penny answered, never very good at figures and hoping Josh hadn't shaded the truth. "It will put you in the clear, darling. Daddy and I had one day of suffering, and we think six weeks is more than enough for you. I'm sure you won't be thoughtless ever again."

"Oh, Mums, I *won't!*"

Parri threw both arms around Penny and said

fervently, "I've learned my lesson. You worried about me when you didn't know where I was, but I've worried about myself in a different way. I've worried about how I was going to *live* for the next two years."

"I know, honey." Penny sighed, then said softly, "I wish you'd never have anything worse in your life, but you will. Growing up is painful but lovely, Parri. If you're steadfast in your ideals and acceptant of punishment for your mistakes, you're building character to meet whatever may come when you're grown. The main thing is to be steadfast and honest with yourself now."

"I know that."

Parri lived with two fundamentally honest people. They were odd sometimes, she thought, a little too old, or too stodgy, or too brilliant to suit her, but they always knew what they were doing and why. "I'll try to remember," she said, cuddling close in a sudden rush of love that made her add, "I don't think I'd have been as noble, Mums, if Davy hadn't made me."

"We thought as much."

Penny laughed softly as she held Parri close. "There aren't many Davys around," she said. "I know one who's called Dave by his friends and Dad by me, and one we call David. I wouldn't be half as honest as I am today if it weren't for them, so you should be grateful that a Davy steered you into a mess of suffering. And now," she said briskly, sure her little talk had gone on 'ong enough to make a permanent groove in Parri's brain, "suppose we discuss your new friend, April. What are we going to do about her?"

"April?" Parri sat up, wondering how her mother could possibly have known she was worried about having abandoned April. Dear, kind April who needed someone to start her on the road to success. "I don't know much to tell you about her," she said.

"You promised to invite her out, didn't you?"

"Yes."

"Then why don't we write and ask her if she'd like to come?"

"Okay."

"At Corridon's, didn't you say?"

"Yes."

"Then let's get up and do it." Penny was ready to rise, but Parri held her down. "It's kind of like this, Mums," she said carefully. "April doesn't know who you and Daddy are. She'd come like a shot if she did, but I don't want her that way. I want her to come to see me, because maybe she liked me. She seemed to. She seemed to think *I* was the one who needed helping. I don't want her to know I think she does. Do you understand, Mums?"

"Yes, I believe I do." Penny nodded thoughtfully before she suggested, "Why don't I write to her mother on my stationery that has simply

Round Tree Farm printed on it, and sign the note Penelope MacDonald. It *is* my name, you know."

"Do you think it would fool her?"

"It should." Penny grinned into her hunched-up knees as she said, "Nobody but my great-grandmother ever called me Penelope, and she only did it because she thought I was named for her. She was the Queen Victoria type, and she willed me a white-gold tiara with three little diamonds in it. She never did know that Grandma and Grandpa named me Penelope because they thought Penny would be a cute nickname. Don't you ever tell anyone," she warned, because she felt so close to Parri, sitting there on the top step with sunlight streaming through the landing window and blending them into one solid shadow on the wall behind them. "I've tried to forget it."

"I wouldn't tell. Perhaps, though, sometimes," Parri said with just a hint of comradely teasing, "I might want to hold it over you. Like when you say in your dignified voice, 'No, Parrish, you may not do it,' I might feel like coming back with, 'Oh now, Penelope, why not?'"

"That would cause a scene." Penny made a face and said, "But let's get back to April. What's her real name, by the way?"

"Mary Schultz." Parri giggled, thinking that Mary Schultz, while not as high-sounding as Penelope Parrish, was equally wrong for a stage name. But she asked. "When shall we invite her?"

"How about Thanksgiving? It comes up next week, and no one in New York ever works from Wednesday evening until Monday morning. It would give her a good, long week end."

"But how about the family?" Parri inquired. "It's always a family time with us."

"We'll let April, or Mary, or whatever name she uses, trot around wherever we go. But I do think," Penny added, feeling that Parri was years younger in her ways than April would turn out to be, "that you should plan some sort of party for her, with boys."

"Now, where would I get any boys?" Parri was aghast at such an idea. She knew the Carter twins down the road, but they weren't as old as she was. Davy was *too* old, and Lang, just the right age, would give April the creeps should he put himself out to be nice to her, which he wouldn't. Lang, Parri secretly thought, was strictly minus.

But her mother was looking at her queerly. "Don't you know any boys?" she asked, suddenly realizing that she had never seen any around.

"No." Parri shrugged and explained, "You don't meet boys in a girls' school. I'd fall dead if any boy but Davy or Lang, and maybe Vance Jordon sometimes, ever spoke to me. I guess we'd better not invite April, huh?" she asked.

"Well, for mercy's sake!" Penny wanted to

jump up and find Josh. She, at fourteen and living on an army post, had known dozens of boys. And living at West Point, where her father was an instructor, boys had always been in and out of the house. But most of them had started coming as David's friends, she remembered. David had been three years older, and whenever he came home a gang came with him. Joshua, at ten, was no good to Parri. Ten-year-old boys were only interested in making spaceships that wouldn't fly. Then she turned to stare at her daughter.

Parri was pretty. She was fourteen and pretty. Her mouth was a little too big, but her face would fill out to fit it, and lipstick might make it her most engaging feature—after her truly gorgeous eyes. "Heavens," she said, wondering why she and Josh had taken Parri out of public school when she reached junior high-school age and put her in Briarcliff. Briarcliff had been fine for Penny Parrish, who lived in a world of cadet uniforms and had an older brother, but not for Parri.

"I do know one boy," Parri brought her back by saying. "He works in the feed store, but he's sort of short and fat. His name's George something-or-other, and he keeps asking me if I'll get your autograph for him."

"He won't do." Penny wondered who would. Who would like Parri for herself alone? "I'll tell you what," she said, confronted by the one problem she had never faced before, finding enough boys for a party. "I'll think about it. You can invite several girls from school to spend the night, and perhaps Davy or Lang can dig up some freshmen from their Academy to come over. But let's settle the problem of April first. She may not want to accept our invitation, you know."

"All right." Parri prayed she would. She wanted April; but with the unexpected chance of knowing some boys, she wanted a party even more. Gosh, she thought, imagine having a party down in the playroom with a lot of boys all over the place! Imagine going from social poverty to being a hostess. Why, she might even be asked to dance! In the new pink party dress and matching satin slippers she had gotten for her birthday. "Let's write the letter quickly!" she cried, springing up.

The stairway seemed a silly place to sit on a Saturday morning. Valuable time was winging by, so she pulled her mother up and hustled her back to her office, where an invitational note was collaborated on and duly written.

April received the heavy gray envelope on Monday morning when she went in to Corridon's to wait for a secretary to call her over to the appointment desk. A whole week had gone by without her name ever having appeared on the bulletin board, so she was surprised to hear the secretary say, "Something for you, April." But instead of being handed a slip of paper which would mean paying the rent, she got a letter.

An invitation to a country weekend. April stood disconsolately holding it, wondering what she should do. Carol was a nice little kid, she remembered, but so what? Who wanted to visit somebody in the country? There were cows out there and miles and miles of nothing. Country! So she thrust the invitation into her worn leather purse, and if her mother hadn't needed some change to buy something at the delicatessen, it might have stayed there forever.

"Look, Mary," her mother said, after they had argued about the invitation for some time, "what've you got to do over Thanksgiving that's better? It's dead in New York—dead, dead, dead. Whyn't you go and take a rest? They must be rich, from the way you described the clothes the girl had on, so why don't you go and find out? I wish somebody would invite me someplace."

So April had finally consented, through pressure and boredom, to reply to Penny's letter by telephone. She would come, she said to Parri, who was ecstatic at the news. She would take the two o'clock bus on Wednesday, since she had no late appointments, and would get wherever it was at three thirty. Would somebody be there to meet her?

Parri cried, "Oh yes!" and wanted to remind April to be sure and bring some country clothes. But it wouldn't be necessary, she was sure. Whatever April brought would be just right. April would know from the ads she did for the fashion magazines. Sometimes the models were shown wearing tweedy suits and looking through field glasses, well braced on their flat-heeled shoes to hold a golden retriever that pulled on its leash. Blitz wasn't exactly a golden retriever, but he was a big country dog, and April would be dressed to match him.

April was coming. That was all that mattered. April would be in a state of shock when she met Penny Parrish and Josh MacDonald; but when she recovered from it, she would be just as excited about the party to be given for her. Boys would flock around April like a school of fish around a shining lure, and there might be a few left over for a pinkish Parri. Not for Carol Gay, just for Parri.

It was a delicious thought, especially since it came after six weeks of no thoughts at all; and Parri hugged it to her, wondering how she would ever live through Tuesday and all the way through Wednesday until late afternoon.

CHAPTER 6

Boys! The subject of boys dominated every conversation in the MacDonald household. Nobody knew any boys. Joshu suggested a few; but since they were all eleven years old or under, they were unacceptable. Parri went about looking despondent, and Penny spent a great deal of time on the telephone, asking her friends if they had friends who had a boy of the partyable age. No one had.

Lang, who might have been some help in the crisis, since he was sixteen and could be pushed into service by his parents, was going off to visit a friend just as soon as the family Thanksgiving dinner would be over. Davy, dropping in late on

Tuesday afternoon with Bitsy, rallied around, but drew blank after blank.

"There just aren't any, Aunt Pen," he said, putting the telephone directory back on the library desk and looking from a dispirited Parri to a disbelieving aunt. "Every guy in Claymore Academy's due to take off for home or somewhere the minute the last class is over, and some'll be let off early so they can catch a certain plane or train. I went there, so I know it's no use trying them. All the high school kids in town are dated up solid. At least so they say," he added. "Let's face it. They don't want to take a chance on coming out here when something better might turn up in town. They don't know Parri."

"And I suppose it would be the same with the girls," Penny said, looking thoughtful, "if we can ever get as far as girls, which we can't."

"I know three," Parri put in. "They're the ones I was going to ask to spend the night. Linda and Debbie Christensen are going to visit Mary Ames, but they aren't much fun. I guess we'd better skip it."

She looked so woebegone and embarrassed that Bitsy moved over to sit beside her on the green-velvet love seat. "Perhaps if you and April come over to our house," she suggested, knowing that her brothers would yell bloody murder, "Neal and Vance will have a gang hanging around." And at that Parri looked startled.

"Neal is twenty-one years old," Parri said, her whole face registering shock, "and Vance is nineteen. They wouldn't want *us*."

"No, I fancy not." Bitsy had to nod agreement, but she did add, "If April seems as old as you say she does, Vance might be decent to her because she's an actress."

"She isn't *that* old." The whole business was hopeless, and Parri knew it. "I guess we'll just have to forget it," she said philosophically, "and do the best we can staying around at home. Maybe if April ever comes back again, I can find enough boys by then to give a party for her. We'll just stick around with the family this time."

And at that, Penny jumped up and flew out of the room.

"Josh!" she cried, finding her husband in the upstairs office and closing the door to lean against it. "We've done something horrible to Parri!"

"We have?" he asked mildly, looking up from the letter he was writing. "What?"

"We've shut her up out here in the country where she doesn't know anybody. We've practically made a *prisoner* of her. Why, the poor child," she said, pushing her hair up and running her fingers through it, "she doesn't have any friends. It's terrible, Josh, just *terrible!*"

"I know it, darling. I've been worrying about it all day." He put the letter aside thoughtfully and motioned her to come sit on his desk.

"We've simply ruined her life," she said, sliding the blotter with her along the polished mahogany.

"I don't think it's quite that bad." Josh smiled as he took her fidgeting hands in his, but he said earnestly, "We've had such a happy life here, Pen, that we didn't realize our Parri is outgrowing it. Last year she was still just a little girl who liked to climb trees with the boys; now she wants to dance with them. Well, that's natural."

"*We* made fudge," Penny said reminiscently, "and had treasure hunts. Parri's never done anything like that. We've neglected her."

"Oh, darling, we haven't. We adore her."

"We've dragged her all over the United States with us," she went right on. "She's met lots of famous people, from the President on down, but she's never had any *fun*. She hasn't, Josh."

"I think she has," he contradicted, "until now."

"Well, what shall we do about *now*?"

"My vote is to send her to high school."

"But it's so far," she protested. "No bus comes near here. I say let's sell this house and move somewhere else."

"Now, Pen, calm down." She was about to plunge off the desk and go pacing about the small room, but he held her and kept the blotter in place. "Nothing's been done to Parri that can't be fixed—not right at the moment, I'll admit not in time for a party, but fairly quickly."

"How?" she demanded.

"By putting her in high school. John can drive her to the bus every morning, or you or I can do it if he has yard work, and we can meet her again in the afternoon. If she has school activities at night, we drive again, that's all. We wait in a drugstore or a movie and bring her back. In a year or two, boys will do it for us."

"That scares me." Penny hid her face in her hands and mumbled, "I don't want Parri to grow up and ride in cars with crazy boys."

"Was David crazy?" he asked. "Is Davy, or Lang?"

"No." Penny shook her head, even though she said from between her fingers, "But Joshu may be. He's always taking chances with his life, and lots of boys may be just like him. I won't know who's a good safe driver."

"Oh, darling," Josh tried not to smile as he said, "all that's a long time from now. That's a bridge we'll have to cross; but Parri—if she's anything like her mother, and I think she is—will pick out the good safe drivers. She's no fool, Penny. And anyway, the problem is *now*."

"Yes." Penny sighed and moved farther back with the blotter. "When should we put her in high school?" she asked acceptantly.

"Next term. February, if they'll take her."

"Oh me." Parri was going to high school. Far, far away to a strange new life. It had been decided, but there was still a loophole. "What if she doesn't want to go?" she asked hopefully.

"Are you trying to be funny?" Josh laughed, but he stood up to kiss her. "Our lives were different from hers, darling," he said, his arms around her waist. "I have a string of orphanages and boardinghouses with my father or my uncle to remember, and you had it the soft way—the easy, delightful, normal way. Parri—well, poor little Parri is burdened with famous parents, but we're going to do the very best we can for her. We knew what we'd be up against when we wanted her. And we knew it about Joshu, too. They're ours, Pen, and it's up to us to see that they get the best."

"I know it." Penny sniffed back a few tears, but she stood up and leaned against him. "Oh, my wise, good Josh," she said into his shoulder. "I'm such a coward, and you're so sane and strong. And—and s-s-smart, too," she stammered.

"Then let's get Parri through this gosh-awful weekend with April," he suggested, knowing her tears would back up when her mind started forward. "Parri doesn't really care about the party —yet. She's just afraid that April might get bored. So let's charm April. Let's make her flip her lid."

"Just flip," Penny corrected.

"Okay. Let's make her flip because she's come to visit an old but helpful couple who can put her where she wants to get."

"Can we do that?"

"Sure. You can investigate her talent and I can shove her in someplace, wherever she fits."

"Thank you, darling. Shall we tell Parri about high school now?"

"Let's wait." Josh was willing to give his daughter everything she deserved, and more, but they had just discounted Parri's disobedience and a seven-hundred-and-fifty-dollar coat, so he said, "She's going to high school if they can take her, but let's not spring it on her yet. Let's not jump the gun. Let it ride a little, Pen—at least that's my advice."

"And it's always good." Penny did slide off the desk this time, but she did it carefully and pushed the blotter back. "We'll wait," she said. "At least until after we talk to the high school principal. When shall we do it?"

"Oh, my impatient Penny. Right after Thanksgiving, if you like."

"I like." She smiled up at him, knowing that a great deal had been settled. Parri was to fly free like Peter Pan, leaving the shadow of a little girl behind. "Gol' darn it," she said, squaring her shoulders, "I guess I'd better go to market."

Whenever theater problems got too much for her, she simply returned to the role of housewife and acted it out. The supermarket always gave her relief: just looking at the well-stocked shelves with their boxes and cans and fancy packaging calmed her. They were so nice and commonplace. Clean, orderly. "I think I'll buy a roast for dinner," she said.

"The stores are closed," Josh's calm voice reminded her, and she turned around.

"I know it, you dope," she retorted. "I can pretend, can't I?" And out she went.

The rest of Tuesday and Wednesday, for the MacDonalds, passed in a fairly peaceful way because they had relinquished all thought of a party —but not for April. Indecision and confusion seemed to be running a race.

One minute she was flatly refusing to go "out in the sticks," and the next she was accepting a pair of shoes, a dress, a hat, from the generous people who lived in the rooming house. And after her mother had finally pushed her and her suitcase out the front door, she sat wretchedly on a bus, wearing a borrowed coat and her mother's pumps.

The coat belonged to Margo Minor, who lived on the third floor and had a steady job in the chorus of a long-running musical. It was black and had a mink collar, but it was four years old and out of style; and April didn't like the way it buttoned tightly down the front, then bunched out over her hips. Not even its mink collar made up for the shiny black fur and jaunty look of Parri's red coat. The pumps had very thin high heels and were just enough too wide to hold her feet steady when she walked. Her dress was her own, a new brown taffeta sheath she had bought wholesale after she modeled it, and everyone said it fitted her as if she had been born in it. The landlady's black patent-leather purse and a new tenant's black kid gloves completed her costume, because, having sprayed her bouffant hairdo until it was glued stiffly in place, she had refused to wear a hat.

So there she sat, staring dully out at nothing. Country. Why had she ever come out here to look at bumpy hills, she asked herself. And cows. Of all the dumb things to do! Sometimes the bus stopped in towns, and she recognized Nyack. She and her sister had danced there in a benefit once, but she had been only eight years old, so couldn't really remember what the place was like. Just a big armory.

She was still thinking about Nyack and wishing she had got off there when the bus pulled in at a curb and the bus driver called back, "Here you are, Miss. Don't forget your suitcase."

She felt glued to the seat. There stood that girl Carol on the sidewalk, the one her mother had called Patty or Parri or something crazy in her letter, and she didn't look at all like the one who had sat on the stool in the drugstore. She had on a camel's hair coat now, and, of all things, woolly white socks that made her look like a country goon. Oh, gosh, let me hide, April was thinking when Parri saw her through the window and waved.

There was nothing to do but get off and bear it, *four whole, long, dull days* of it, so she pulled her suitcase down from the rack and teetered along the aisle to the door of the bus.

"Oh, hello!" Parri cried, looking up eagerly. "I'm so glad you've come! Here, let me have your bag so you can jump off. And watch out for the bottom step, it's awfully high."

The worn case changed hands; and by clinging to the handrail beside the door, April was able to swing herself down without tearing the seams in her too-tight skirt. "Hello," she said, wishing the bus wouldn't go away and leave her. It had become familiar by now, and this excited girl was a stranger.

"This is John," Parri was saying, passing the suitcase along to a middle-aged man who looked as if he had seen better days.

He wore a short coat that April was sure was at least ten years older than hers and a red wool cap with dangling earflaps. He even wore rubber boots caked with mud, and he said, "Howdy," just like a poor farmer on TV. April wondered if he could be a relative.

"John drove me in," Parri was explaining as she led the way to a station wagon that looked more like what April had expected, long and rich. "I wanted to meet you all by myself so we could talk a little about our wonderful day in New York. Wasn't it fun?"

"If you thought so."

"I loved it." Parri waited while April slid carefully onto the second seat in the car, smoothed her coat under her, and pulled her skirt over her knees; then she ran around and hopped in from the other side. "I think it was the most exciting day I've ever had," she said, punching John in the back to tell him they were ready to move.

"Did you get the part?" April didn't care one way or the other, but she knew she should make conversation.

"Well, yes and no." Parri hesitated, then said bluntly, wanting to be honest, "I think I could have had it, April. I wanted you to get it, but you didn't."

"Think nothing of it." April shrugged and added, "I'll get a lot of better offers. I had four modeling jobs last week. Junior-deb ones, too."

"Oh, I'm glad. Were they for the good magazines?"

"Yes." April proudly ticked off the fashion publications and was describing the dresses she had worn when she suddenly broke off to ask, "Why didn't you take it—the part, I mean."

"Well, you see, my parents are very strict—about the theater, that is. They're simply wonderful about everything else, but they think I'm too young to be an actress."

The car was on a winding country road now, and Parri looked out to explain, "We have relatives living all around here. If you look out your window, you can see my aunt's and uncle's house way over there in the distance."

April obediently followed Parri's gaze and saw nothing but a pasture where dozens of contented cows were grazing. There were a few fine, trim horses separated from them by a fence, but none of the horses was as good-looking as the ones the New York mounted police rode. "It's nice," she said, holding on as the station wagon took a sharp right turn.

Parri, who had known where to look, had seen the great mansion of Gladstone in the distance, but she pointed to a neat white clapboard house in a yard near the edge of the road and said, "My grandmother and grandfather live there. Our house is coming up around the next bend."

"Oh." April was surprised when they drove between high wooden gateposts topped with lanterns and stopped before the largest house she had ever been invited to enter.

"Welcome to Round Tree Farm," Parri cried, springing out and dragging the suitcase with her.

She didn't know exactly what she thought of April. She was April, yet she wasn't. She looked more like April Showers than Parrish MacDonald looked like Carol Gay, but she wasn't very lively or enthusiastic about anything. Not like she had

103

been in New York. She acted as if this whole business bored her. Parri secretly wondered why April had bothered to come. With New York so gay and glamorous, why had she accepted such a dull invitation? "Come meet Mums and Daddy," she said, holding back a sigh as she plunked the suitcase down in the hall. And she led the way to the living room, saying, "Here are my mother and father, April. Mums, Daddy, this is April Showers."

April, advancing with polite resignation, froze in the middle of the beige carpet. Surely . . . oh no! "Oh, my goodness!" she gasped, sure she was in the middle of a daydream. It couldn't be Penny Parrish coming toward her in a powder-blue skirt and matching sweater! Not with a little white collar under her chin and flat-heeled brogues. It couldn't be. "How—how do you do," she gulped, staring past Penny's outstretched hand at a perfect copy of the man everybody in the theatrical world tried to meet, and few could. Then something in her brain snapped like the shutter of a camera and took a picture. "Why, you're—you *are!*" she cried. "Parrish—MacDonald—why, you are!"

"Of course we are." Penny smiled and let her hand find April's as it fluttered around in the air. "Parri didn't want to tell you, dear," she said, "because she wanted you to like her for herself. We're so glad you did and came to visit her."

"And us, too," Josh said, in welcome, smiling down at her in the kind warm way the unimportant people of Broadway never got to see. And then, understanding her flustered state, he said, "Parri, suppose you take April up to your room and settle her in and explain your double life. She deserves some briefing."

"Yes sir, proper service coming up." Parri had the suitcase again and was ready to ring up the curtain on another scene. This one had been better than the first one, so her hopes rose. April had been stunned. She had been plain knocked out. And she still was. She still stood center stage, committing the actor's unforgivable sin, which is going blank and not coming up with a line. "April," she prompted, tugging, "come on. Mums and Dad won't go away. You'll have days and days to see them around, so come on!"

"Thank you." April looked at both Penny and Josh and wondered if she should back away from their royal presences. She should bow as she backed, she thought, or at least let go of Penny's hand. Hers would never be the same again, and she would never wash where Penny Parrish had touched it; but she couldn't stand there clinging to a famous actress forever. "Golly," she said, "I mean, well, thank you for inviting me." And she did move backward after all, because Parri pulled her from behind by the bunchy gathers of her coat.

She went up the stairway beside Parri, the suitcase bumping between them, but on the landing she stopped and looked through the big windows at a woods and rippling brook. "Oh, my gosh," she said. "I think you were mean not to tell me Penny Parrish and Josh MacDonald were your parents. I was so embarrassed."

"I didn't mean to fool you," Parri tried to explain, "not at the time. I just wanted to be like everybody else. Can't you understand, April?"

"Yes, I guess so. You won't believe this," April said, "but I've never been in a real house before. Apartments and boardinghouses are all I've ever seen, except for a couple of times when Mom and I've gone to visit a cousin who lives in Jersey City. Her house is in the middle of a long row, though, and just has windows on the front and back, and she rents out the upstairs. I never knew anyone who lived in a whole big house."

"Well, we do—all over it." Parri couldn't conceive of living any other way. This had always been her home; and while she had lived in apartments and hotels when her mother played in New York, she had always come back to the country on weekends. Even in California they had rented a house.

"This is my room," she said, when April had mounted the last six steps and walked carefully along the carpeted hall. "Come on in and take off your coat."

106

April stopped just inside the door. "Why, it's the most beautiful room I ever saw," she said, looking at pink dimity counterpanes on white twin beds, at long pink draperies at the four windows, at padded chairs, a white desk and dressing table. First Penny Parrish and now this! She felt as if she had accidentally rubbed Aladdin's lamp. Things were going too fast.

"All the furniture used to be my mother's when she was young," Parri answered, having hoped she would get a more modern set for Christmas. "My Aunt Tippy used it after Mums got married, and then Grandma and Grandpa decided that it should belong to me and sent it over."

"I never had a room of my own." April watched Parri plop the suitcase on a window seat in a nest of lacy pillows, then scuff off her shoes and sit cross-legged on one of the pink-counterpaned beds. "Once I did, for two weeks, when my sister Violet went on tour with a road show," she said, "but the show flopped and Violet came back. Mom and I share a room now that Violet's married and lives in Flatbush. It must be fun to have a room where you can close your door and be by yourself."

"I guess it is." For the last six weeks Parri had thought of her room as a jail; but now, seeing wistful little April looking as if she had floated into a pink heaven on a pink cloud, she asked, "Would you like to have the guest room, April? It can be all yours, and you can be alone in it whenever you come to visit me. It's right across the hall. Come, I'll show it to you."

She was about to hop up again, but April darted across the room and stopped her. "I think I'd rather stay in here with you," she said. "I'm a little scared, and this way it would be sort of like going away to boarding school, I think. I always wanted to go, but Mom never could afford it. We could talk and sort of kid around in here, couldn't we?"

"Why, I guess so." April seemed so suddenly changed to Parri. She liked everything. She wasn't glamorous or pert. She was just a girl—too blond, too thin, too overdressed.

"I didn't know what I was getting into," April said, taking off her coat and revealing herself in the form-fitting brown silk. "I still don't." And then she smiled her engaging grin that had captured Parri in New York. "But whatever it is," she said, "I like it. I'm all wrong and my clothes are all wrong for out here—I knew that the minute I saw your mother and you—but I'll do the best I can, if you'll help me." She walked over to her suitcase and snapped the catches, then lifted the lid. "I guess your friends will think I'm a mess," she said, looking down on a dotted wool dress that had a bunchy crinoline folded inside it.

"My—my friends?" Parri had listened to April's

apologies with a feeling of self-importance and complacency. April had thought she led a wonderful life; April had envied her and compared her own meager existence with that of the fortunate Miss Parrish MacDonald's. But now an unexpected admission of her own had to be made. She wasn't as all-important as she had thought she was. "I don't have any friends," she admitted, swinging her feet over the side of the bed and bracing herself with her hands. "You don't want to go to a girls' boarding school, April. I know, because I go to one. I wanted to give a party for you, but—because of the boarding school—I don't know any boys."

"Boys?" April turned around and grinned. "Who does know any boys?" she asked. "And who needs them anyway?"

"Don't you know boys?"

"Sure." April shook out the dotted dress and laid it over the chair as she said, "Loads of boys go to my school. But all of them either have acting jobs at night, or are trying to get jobs, or else they hot-foot it off to soda-jerk somewhere. The kids in my school never see each other after they finish classes, and they never talk anything but shop while they're there. The only boy I really know lives in our boardinghouse, and he works for a wholesale furrier during the daytime and takes acting lessons, and fencing lessons, and dancing lessons at night. So you see I don't know any boys either, and I certainly haven't time for them."

"Oh, good." A great relief flooded over Parri. April didn't know what fun the average teen-ager had. But what would she do out here? How would she fill four evenings and three days in the country? "I'm afraid you'll get bored," she said.

"Me?" April laughed and let the dresses wait while she turned around to say, "I won't get bored in *this* house, kid. When I'm not staring at your mother and father and trying to think of something to say to them, I'll just be walking around. It would take me days and days of walking around in this house—going up and down the stairs, and finding out where all the hallways go— to get tired of it. I can have a perfectly swell time just going out the front door and coming in the back. Don't worry about me."

"Oh, April!" Parri did spring off the bed then and she and April hugged each other. Each had learned a great deal about a different side of life, and April was the first to put it into words.

"We're not a bit alike," she said. "I wouldn't want to be you and you couldn't ever be me, but I think we're going to like each other. I don't know how much meeting Penny Parrish has to do with the way I feel now, but I feel changed inside. Sort of honest. Parri, I didn't have four jobs last week. I didn't get any, so don't tell your folks I did."

"I won't," Parri promised. "They won't care, and they won't even ask."

"Let's forget business. I didn't come here to drum up any, so—well . . ."

"We'll play it by ear." Parri laughed, and realizing how lucky she was, she flew about helping April unpack her suitcase.

CHAPTER 7

"THAT GIRL'S OKAY," Davy said to Parri, looking the length of Gladstone's long drawing room at April, who sat on the floor playing tiddlywinks with Carli and Joshu.

April wore the wool dress that had spots as big as silver dollars on a black background, but the crinoline had been taken out and a full white petticoat of Parri's substituted.

"I don't want to look too fussy," April had said that morning, brushing and brushing the stiffness out of her hair so it would fall softly around her face. "I have to in New York," she explained, working on a roughed-up tangle that refused to lie down, "but I caught on right away that it's all wrong out here. I'm not so dumb." And she had gratefully accepted Parri's petticoat and put on the ballet slippers she had brought to wear with her quilted bathrobe.

She looked cute sitting on the carpet, her legs stuck straight out like a doll's, the tip of her tongue caught between her teeth, her cheeks pink with the excitement of snapping a plastic disk into a glass cup. She had been excited all day, after she had recovered from the shock of driving up to an impressive country mansion and having a real live butler take her coat. And she had been shy. Shy and polite, and eager to do whatever anyone suggested. The slang and shrugs had vanished with the too-tight dress and high-heeled shoes that had been hidden away in her suitcase. April seemed as changeable as the month whose name she had taken.

"Mums likes her," Parri said, watching April too. "We didn't have anything special to do last night, so Mums and Daddy sort of worked with her, coaching her, you know. Daddy says the play we tried out for needs an understudy for the three young parts, and he said—if April's willing to let her hair go back to being brown like mine, or at least dye it a little darker—he's sure he can get her the job."

"Would you feel bad about it?" Davy looked quizzically at her, but she shook her head.

"At first I didn't like it much," she said. "I was jealous, I suppose, just sitting there and watching my own parents do something for a stranger they wouldn't do for me. And then I realized that I've plenty of time. And I've already learned the simple things they were teaching April, just from watching Mums rehearse a part with Daddy coaching her. When I'm ready, I'll have Mums and Daddy back of me—but April hasn't anybody." Parri grinned and said, "You know, I got so I felt like an agent. April was my 'property,' and I was selling her."

She was silent as she recalled a little scene that had taken place when she and April were getting ready for bed. She was already under her pink electric blanket when April, her face scrubbed shinning clean of make-up, had run over to kneel down beside her. "Thank you, Parri," she had said. "I *loathed* coming out here, and I thought you were awfully klunky when I first saw you. Now I'm so grateful, I could cry."

"Don't," Parri had answered, feeling embarrassed because April's face looked so naked. "I wasn't sure I liked you so much either."

"Were you ashamed of me?"

"A little. I couldn't remember exactly what you looked like when I invited you, and when I saw you I wondered what I would do with you. I felt sort of puffed up and important when I introduced you to Mums and Daddy—almost superior. But when you told me you'd never had a room of your own and didn't know any boys, everything was suddenly all right. I liked you the way I had in New York, only differently. I liked you just as a—a *girl*."

"Thanks a lot." April had climbed into her bed and snuggled down under her own pink blanket, and Parri had snapped off the light.

"You see," she said now to Davy, who was grinning because Lang had gotten into the tiddlywinks game, "I'll never get to see the side of life April knows. I'll never visit her in New York because she hasn't any room for me, but she can come out here and we can have fun." She stopped to sigh, then said, "Oh dear, I don't know what fun it will be. I wish I knew some boys."

"It's too bad, but you don't." Her words had reminded Davy that if he didn't hustle over to Bitsy Jordon's before a fellow from Pennsylvania got there, he might find himself the sturdy, uninteresting base of a triangle. Keith Drayton was just as attractive in his way as Bitsy was in hers, and to hold up a romance that leaned toward an apex above him was like being the strong man in an acrobatic act. No glory in that. "I'd better take her somewhere," he said aloud, to Parri's surprise, and away he went.

The whole day seemed to pass with people leaving and coming back, with Parri kissing some of them good-bye, then discovering them back in the house again. Even Lang. It was four o'clock before he drove away in his father's sports

car, with everyone waving to him—even April—
and ten minutes later he reappeared down in the
game room to find his red hunting jacket and
shotgun.

"Nobody goes hunting in the *city!*" Parri cried,
missing the shot her Uncle David lobbed across
the table-tennis net. And she got a black look
from Lang for an answer.

"I don't understand anything," she said that
night to April, lying under her electric blanket.
"You've never known any boys, yet Lang waited
to drive you home from Gladstone."

"He drove you too," April answered, pinning up
her hair at the dressing table. "I think he did it
because he's your cousin. And, anyway," she
cried, jumping up and spinning around, "it doesn't
matter. I had the most *wonderful* day!"

"Ugh," Parri said, fed up with family gatherings. "What was so wonderful about it?"

"Well, first, just being in a house like that. I
never believed any house could be so grand unless it was on a movie set. And being with people
who loved each other; and playing games; and
sitting at a great long table of relatives all eating
together—not like in a boardinghouse, where
everybody grabs and talks shop. But most of all,"
she said, sitting on the edge of Parri's bed and
rerolling a curl that had fallen down, "I think it
was watching your mother. She was always seeing
that everyone else was having a good time. I

didn't think famous actresses ever gave a hoot about what other people did. I decided a long time ago that I'd be hard and mean when I got to be famous. I changed a lot of my plans today."

"What others?" Parri asked, curious.

"Why, you don't have to be snobbish just because you're rich." April thought a moment before she said, "Take your Aunt Carrol. I guess she's about as rich as anyone would ever want to be, yet she's perfectly lovely. I think she's the loveliest lady I ever saw. I'd like to be as great an actress as your mother and as sweet as your Aunt Carrol. I'd like to be you," April said, taking down the curl again and turning the roller around and around between her fingers. "You've got everything, Parri. Believe me, I know. If you and Davy and Lang, and the little kids too, don't turn out as good as you ought to, you won't ever be able to go to a psychoanalyst and say, 'Look what my childhood did to me.' Lots of people blame everything on their childhood, but you can't—not ever."

"I don't plan to," Parri answered, unable to see herself lying on a couch telling her troubles to a stranger. "But there are times when . . ."

"Oh, yeah," April broke in, reverting to her caustic slanginess. "I'll just bet. Some night when Mom's going off to visit in Jersey City I'll invite you to come in and spend the night with me. You try it for one night, and you'll see how good you've got it. I don't mean because we're poor," she said, loving her mother who could never quite make ends meet. "but because . . ." she looked at innocent little Parri in neat pin curls before she said roughly, ". . . because nobody in that whole darned boardinghouse ever had the breaks to get to the top or the courage to admit that he isn't good enough to get there on his own. You won't have to worry either way, Parri. You've got it made if you want it."

"I suppose so."

Parri knew how easy her life was. It was like an embroidery pattern made on a sewing machine. All she had to do was follow the markings and repeat the pattern over and over. The machine kept right on going. She wanted to say something like that to April, but it seemed too foolish. April would neither understand nor accept it. So she only nodded.

The next three days were a delightful change, because April had thrown aside her own laborious pattern and was thoroughly enjoying a playtime. They went to Highland Falls and giggled over malted milks; they made a tour of West Point, with John driving them and not caring how many statues they stopped to inspect or how long they stayed in the one hotel. They sat in the coffee shop of the hotel, pretending they were going to a dance that night and discussing the dresses they would wear, the kind of corsages they wanted, and whether they should walk along

Flirtation Walk if their dates suggested it. And April, who hadn't known where the United States Military Academy was located or exactly what it was, had more ideas of what they should do and see than Parri. And then it was inevitably Sunday afternoon, and April was back on the bus.

She had taken off the navy-blue skirt and sweater Parri had lent her, reluctantly folding them and laying them on top of the borrowed storm coat, and had put on her own brown silk and tight coat. But her hair was still as flyaway as Parri's, and she had hopped on the bus without caring how she made it or what ripped in the process.

"Good-bye," she called down, wishing she had a picture of the whole MacDonald family as they stood below her, not to show and brag about, but to keep forever. "Thank you a million times. I've never had such a wonderful time!" The door closed, the bus began to move, and she could only wave.

"I hope it isn't going to be dull for you, honey," Parri heard her mother say, when she was blinking back tears and swallowing great gulps of cold air while she tried to keep from crying. "I think you should bring one of the girls from Briarcliff home on weekends."

"I'd rather have April," Parri answered. "We're both planning to have a career someday, and we have more in common."

"But April may not be able to come," her father reminded. "If I can get her the understudy job, she'll be working."

"She shouldn't *have* to!" Parri declared hotly. "She shouldn't have to work so hard at her age. Why, she doesn't have any more fun than *I* do!"

Penny and Josh looked at each other, and Penny signaled, "Shall we tell her about going to high school?" But Josh shook his head, and she knew it meant, "Not yet. We'd better wait till we talk to the principal and have something definite." So Parri walked lonesomely back to the car.

Teachers, like everyone else, must have their vacations; but Penny, finding the office of the high school closed on Friday, had rattled the doorknob and fumed because schools don't operate on a steady six-day-a-week basis. "Theaters do," she had said to Josh, who was watching her peek through a pane of frosted glass into an obviously empty office. "*We* don't knock off for holidays. Oh, darn it!" She had given the knob one last irritated rattle, then had followed him out, still looking hopefully back.

"You won't have to be lonesome much longer, honey," she promised now, ignoring Josh's warning to just a small extent; and Parri gave her a frozen look.

"Thank you too much," she said. "You make me feel like Grandma. I'll have my memories to live on. One long weekend." Then she leaned against the car and said, "That's not a bad name for a play. It sounds pretty dramatic, and people wouldn't know until they got inside the theater that it was only about a couple of teen-age girls who had a heyday with the family. You might produce it, Daddy, and give me my cut on its one performance."

"Oh Parri, darling."

Penny hugged her unhappy daughter, but Joshu scowled and said, "Oh, my gosh. How creepy can you get?" And they all silently took their accustomed seats in the station wagon.

CHAPTER 8

Parri went back to school on Monday. All the girls were chattering about their holiday. Almost all agreed that it had been simply fabulous; a few said it was dull; and some, like Parri, labeled it "so-so."

Parri's best friends wanted to know about April, but she didn't know what to tell them. They never could have understood April, had she wanted to tell them about her, because there was the April who came and the April who left. How could she make them see the astounding change that had taken place in between? So she merely said, "She was lots of fun," and let it go at that. And on Tuesday night April telephoned.

"I got the understudy job!" she cried. "All three

of the juvenile parts, even one for a girl who is older than I am and for a boy who can be switched to a girl if he has to be—and I owe it all to you. Oh, Parri, I *do!*" she repeated, when Parri sent a meek protest along the wire. "I'm so excited, I could dance up and down!"

"I'm glad," Parri answered, trying not to feel jealous. She didn't want the understudy job, but she felt dull and left out. She wanted something exciting to tell, too. Anything.

"And I'm to rehearse all this week," April went on. "In fact, I began today. My salary's starting as of now, and after next week I can model in the daytime."

"I'm glad," Parri said again; and she asked, "You won't be coming out this weekend, will you?"

"My goodness, no." April's satisfied laugh floated along the wire like bubbles. "I'll have to be at the theater for the Saturday matinee and at night, you know. Somebody might get sick, and I'd have my big chance. Do you think you could come in and have lunch with me a week from next Saturday? By then I can afford to take you to a better place than the drugstore."

"I'm almost sure I can't. I can't come in for a long time," Parri said; and she added sadly, "school, you know."

April was gone forever, and she knew it. There had been such a brief interlude of April. Just a

123

few days, like the hint of spring her name promised; and then, instead of summer following spring, it was winter again. Had Parri hopefully doubted it, she was sure when April said, "Call your father to the phone, will you? I want to thank him, and your mother too, if she isn't busy. I want to tell them all about what's happened to me."

"I'll call them." Parri held the receiver away from her ear, then said carefully into its mouthpiece, "Good-bye, April," and laid it down on the library desk.

And so the days went on. Wednesday, Thursday, Friday, with Parri coming home from school or stopping off to spend a few hours with some of her relatives, hunting Davy who was never home, and avoiding Carli who always was. And finally it was Saturday afternoon; and with nothing better to do, she rode to town with John, who had errands there.

"I'll go in and talk to Uncle Bobby, then meet you at the hardware store," she said, climbing down from the high pickup truck in front of a brick building that had gasoline pumps at the side and a sign on top saying PARRISH MOTORS. "Will half an hour be long enough?"

"Nope." John shifted gears while he called, "I've got a lot to do. I'll hunt you up."

"All right." Parri knew she could sit in her uncle's office until kingdom come if she didn't mind the boredom. "I'll be right here," she said, and walked across a cement space and into a showroom where three fine, shiny cars were on display.

She looked at the cars for some time, wishing she owned the blue convertible and could take off in it on strange, fascinating roads; then went along a corridor to what her uncle called his "executive suite."

"Hi, Uncle Bobby," she said, stopping in the door and addressing the top of a head showing above an old-fashioned roll-top desk that Bobby Parrish had found in a secondhand store. "I've come to call on you."

"Have a seat." Feet came down from the desk, and a swivel chair shot upright as the napping owner of the agency leaned over to lift some automobile advertisements from one of the red-leather chairs his wife had insisted he should have for customers. "What brought *you* in?" he asked, piling the folders on his already cluttered desk.

"John had things to do, and I didn't," she said, sitting carefully on the part of the seat that wasn't dusty.

Bobby was her youngest uncle and, to her, the most interesting one. He was blond and blue-eyed like her Uncle David, but his eyes were the blue of a summer morning's sky through which a few of last night's naughty stars peeped out. She knew he could be serious when he wanted to be, because he had convinced Susan Jordon that he was steady enough to marry and was doing amazingly well with his agency, but most of the time he was young and entertaining. "I just thought I'd like to talk to you," she said.

"Good. About anything special?"

His feet were back on his desk, showing he had plenty of time to give her, so she shook her head and said, "No."

"How's school?" he asked, to make conversation.

"Very ungood."

"You had a cute little weekend guest. Is she coming back soon?"

"No, I don't think so. She—well, Daddy got her a part in a play, so she'll be busy from now on and, anyway she'd be bored too death out here." Parri stopped and gave a faltering smile before she said, "It's so awfully *dull* out in the middle of the country."

"Could be, at your age." Bobby had the gift of reading more in people's speeches than the speaker realized. He could tell when a customer was beginning to weaken, when Susan was about to explode because he was being unreasonable and messy, even when it was time to stop heckling David or Penny. He hadn't heckled Penny for a long time, he thought, watching Parri closely, but he'd better take another shot at it. It was up to her to see that Parri had some fun. "I suppose you'll be going to a party or a dance tonight," he said, testing.

"Of course not," Parri answered. "My goodness, who would ever ask me to a party out here? The girls dance together at school on Saturday nights, because you have to be a junior before you can go to the Claymore Academy dances."

"I seem to remember something about that," he said, grinning. "My child bride went to Claymore hops when I was at the Point. That was when she said I was too old for her," he explained, knowing that his and Susan's years of arguments had been open discussion in the family, so setting about to entertain his lonely little guest with anecdotes. "Why, once she . . ." Then he sat up and looked over the top of his desk. "Yes, Mose," he said. "What is it?"

A boy a little older than Parri stood in the doorway, holding a sheet of paper. He had gray eyes and neutral-colored hair, and fitted compactly into a plaid flannel shirt and faded jeans. He startled Parri, but looked like an opportune victim to Bobby.

"It's the invoice, sir," he said. "Mr. Cantrelli wants you to sign it."

"Sure, bring it in."

Bobby reached up for the paper and said casually, "This is Mosely Carson, Parri, but everybody calls him Mose. And this is my niece, Mose, Parri MacDonald."

127

"Hello," they said together, studying each other briefly. Then Bobby gave the paper back, and Mose said, "It's nice to know you, Parri," and went out.

Parri seemed dazed by her short encounter with a boy. She stared at the empty doorway for some seconds before she said, "My goodness, Uncle Bobby, I never expected to see such a gorgeous hunk of man in here."

Bobby Parrish had never considered Mose a gorgeous hunk of anything, but he said, "His father's a colonel, stationed at the Point, and Mose works for me on Saturdays."

"I've never seen him before."

"He's usually back in the shop."

Sometimes on Saturday mornings, Bobby had watched Mose whistle softly while he worked. He always seemed so completely happy that Bobby often wondered what he thought about. Was he planning to take the path of least resistance and follow his father's career, as the Parrish boys had? And one morning he had asked him.

"What do you plan to do when you finish high school, Mose?" he had inquired. "Go to the Academy?"

"No, sir." Mose had spoken up promptly, and his slow engaging grin had spread. "I'm shooting for the diplomatic service," he'd said. And Bobby was surprised.

"How come," he asked, "when you have an army background?"

"Well, sir, it's like this." Mose laid his wrench on the fender of the car he was working on, and said, "We've kicked around over the world a lot—the family, I mean—and I've seen some things that made me think this country sure could use some good diplomats—fellows who've really studied for the job and can keep track of the score. I think we're badly needed, sir."

"Yes, I suppose so." Bobby wished Mose would drop the "sir." It made him feel as if he had been out of the army fifty years instead of two, but he only asked, "How are you at languages?"

"Pretty fair, sir. I speak good German from having lived in Germany two years, and I'm taking French at school, and one of the tacs up at the Point is tutoring me in Spanish at night. I figure I ought to have a pretty good start for college. However," he said ruefully, "with things the way they're going now, the State Department will probably send me to Russia or the Far East. Fortunately for me, I picked up some Japanese when Dad was stationed there, and I'm boning up on it in my spare time."

Bobby thought of that conversation now, while he watched Parri watch the door. Mose is one boy in a hundred, he thought; and he surprised them both by suggesting, "Why don't we take him home to dinner with us?"

129

"Mose?" Parri looked pleased, then resigned. "He won't go," she said. "He'll have a date tonight."

"He'll have a date with my gas pumps," Bobby replied, delighted with himself in the role of benefactor. He would teach Penny a thing or two, he thought. She might be a big wheel in the theater world, but she hadn't the wits to go out and find friends for Parri. All the great Mr. Parrish had to do was to recognize a problem, then pay someone overtime to work his pumps. "Mose will leave and come back when I tell him to," he said.

"All right. Let's go get him." Parri was for capturing Mose then and there, but Bobby shook his head.

"Six o'clock," he decreed, not wanting to risk more money than he had to on a long shot. "He'll stay on here till six, and I'll give him an extra hour till eight. Okay?"

"Yes, but I don't look very dressed up," Parri answered, wishing she had worn her red wool instead of just a school skirt and a sweater. "I'd go home and dress, if I had anyone to take me and bring me back in time."

"You look fine," Bobby told her, looking her over critically—not as his niece, but as a girl with whom he might have been ordered to spend a couple of hours when he was fifteen.

She passed by a narrow margin, because even then he had had definite ideas about "his type of woman." He had thought little Alcie Jordon to be the personification of all virtues, so why shouldn't Parri see this future ambassador as really something? "I'll drive you home and bring you back," he said, sure it was what Susan would want him to do. Susan would know how important the right dress and nylons and fancy sandals were. "I'll tell Mose, and then we'll get going before somebody comes in and wants to buy a couple of dozen cars."

Parri was so excited when she was back in Bobby's showroom, waiting for Mose, that she couldn't have told how many cars were still there. She had left a scribbled note for her mother that read, "Have gone to Uncle Bobby's to dinner. There'll be a boy there." And if Minna had wondered why she swished out with a flash of red showing beneath her last-year's Sunday coat, Parri had had no time to stop and explain. She was merely breathing until it was time for things to begin.

"Here I am, sir," Mose said to Bobby, who had gone to sleep in one of the cars. He still wore his jeans and plaid shirt, but he was scrubbed clean. And he added, "Mac has taken over the pumps until I come back."

"Good." Bobby pulled himself out of the car and drove them home.

"Susan?" he called, parking in the garage and hustling them through an empty kitchen and dining room, to the center hall. "Susan? We've got company. Hey, Daffy-dilly, where are you?"

"Coming." Susan ran down the stairs, holding their daughter in her arms. "Well, hi," she said, having been briefed by a telephone call. "What fun!" And she handed the baby to Bobby. "You take her—I'm tired of her," she said, kissing him over the top of the baby's head, "and I think she's tired of me. We're just plain bored with each other and we welcome new faces."

She led the way into the living room, and it amused Parri to watch Bobby flop down in a comfortable chair and plunk his daughter on his knees. Bobby had never cared much for his nieces and nephews when they were small, except to tease them, and Parri could still remember her fright when he threw her high in the air and caught her just before she hit the ground. But this baby? He hugged her in a rough, endearing way, and called her Princess.

"We haven't got a name for her yet," he said, trying to pull the baby loose from his necktie. "Of course she's Elizabeth Marjorie Parrish, for Susan's mother and mine, but we've got more Elizabeths around than you can shake a stick at, and Mom says if we call her Marjorie she'll kill us."

He was rough, yet gentle; and when Susan came to take the baby to bed, he asked, "Why can't she eat with us? She always does."

"Because we have company," she said, holding out her arms. "No one wants to eat with a messy mess in a high chair. Give her to me."

But Bobby only looked down at his daughter, who said, "Me, me, me," and prepared to slide off his lap and toddle to the dining room on unsteady legs.

"She sure is stupid," he said to Mose, who had offered his wristwatch for a toy and was sitting on the floor, legs folded under him, dangling it. "Other kids talk when they're a year old. They say 'mama' and 'daddy.' But what does *she* say? Nothing, except 'me, me, me.'"

"They even tried calling her Me for a while," Parri explained, "because it seemed to suit her, but every time they said, 'Give it to Me,' they handed things to each other. It got confusing."

"Well, give Me to me," Susan said, laughing. "The dinner's getting cold, so we'll have to put up with her. Parri, honey, you know where to sit, and Mose, you can take the only seat that's left, except the high chair."

Everyone talked during dinner. The baby contentedly pushed a few peas around and around on the tray of her high chair, and after Parri had helped clear the table and they had finished their dessert, Susan said, "Time for bed, Miss Parrish."

"I'll go along and help you," Bobby offered, giving her a gentle nudge to say it would be thoughtful to leave Parri and Mose alone for a few minutes. "You never do pin her in to suit me."

Parri could hear them arguing and laughing as they went up the stairs; and when she and Mose were back in the living room, she asked, "Would you like to go down to the playroom and put on some records?"

"Not unless you would," he said. "I had an idea during dinner, but I never did find the right time to bring it out in the open. It's about a nickname for Mr. and Mrs. Parrish's baby."

"What kind of nickname?"

He was standing in front of the fireplace, and as a burning log fell forward, he moved the screen and pushed it back with the toe of his shoe. "Well," he said, replacing the screen and turning around, "the Haitians have a way of calling their kids Ti- something or other. I noticed it when I was down there on the Point Four mission with Dad. Ti means 'little' in Creole. It's spelled *t-i*, but it's pronounced *tee*, and it's put in front of the name: Ti Joe, Ti Pierre, Ti Rose. Maybe if the Parrishes would say Ti Me they'd know which one they're talking about."

"Why, it's wonderful!" Parri went dashing out to the foot of the stairway and called upward, "Hey, up there. Mose has a name for Elizabeth. Come where I can see you and I'll tell you. It's simply out of this world!"

"Hm?" Susan looked down with a safety pin in her mouth. "Whaw is?" she asked around it.

"The name. Ti Me. Ti means 'little' in Creole, he said, so you can call her Ti Me."

"Perfect." Susan took the pin out of her mouth and cried, "Wait till I tell Bobby! Ti Me shot soapsuds all over the front of his shirt, and he's changing it. We'll be down in a minute." And they could hear her calling as she went along the hall, "Bobby, she's got a name. Ti Me has a name. Mose thought of it."

"They're crazy about it," Parri said, hurrying back to the living room. "But you heard Susan. Aren't you proud to have named the boss's baby?"

"Well, I guess so." He watched her drop into a deep chair, her full skirt billowing out over a peeking edge of white lace, her curls as brown and shining as her eyes, and said, "Sure, I'm glad, but it's funny I haven't seen you around before."

"Oh, I never get around." Parri laughed, then a little frown appeared between her brows, and she asked, "Weren't you in the sixth grade when I was in the fifth?"

"Hunhuh. We just came last year."

"Oh." She nodded her head and said, "I don't know why I feel as if I'd known you before. I couldn't have, because I've never even been in the high school!"

"I went in as a freshman."

"And that makes you a sophomore now." Parri

sighed, then brightened. "I'm going to high school next year," she said, forgetting that she had never discussed the matter with her parents. "There's going to be an awful fuss about it at home," she added, "but I'm going."

"I really am going," she repeated, to reassure herself. Then she asked, "Do you think I should?"

"Why, sure, if you want to. It's a darned good high school." Mose sat down, too, and clasped his hands between his long thin legs in their tight jeans. "It would be swell if you do," he said, thinking that she would brighten up a classroom. And then he suddenly asked, "What are you doing tomorrow?"

"Sunday?" Parri looked startled. "Oh my, I wish you hadn't asked me that," she said, not understanding. "It's such a dreary day."

"Why?"

"Because after church, we always go to Aunt Carrol's and Uncle David's for middle-of-the-day dinner. The whole family of us—even Ti Me." Parri smiled when she said the baby's new name, but sobered again to say, "And we stay all afternoon. Mums always takes old clothes for Joshu, so he can go outdoors and mess around. Davy goes off to ride his horse, and Lang goes somewhere with his friends, and Carli goes to play with the gardener's child. I read a while, then Grandpa gets up from his nap, and Davy comes back. If it's summer, we all go outside to play tennis and have tea; and if it's winter . . ." She broke off to say apologetically, "I didn't mean to make such a speech."

"Go on," he urged. "It sounds like something out of a book."

"It is. Daddy calls it 'the gathering of the clan.' Well," she thought for a moment as if she had lost the thread of her recounting, then said, "That's almost the end of it, thank goodness. Aunt Susan brings Ti Me down from her nap, and we start getting ready to go home. That takes about an hour, because Ti Me keeps holding out her arms and saying, 'Me, me, me,' and everybody has to carry her around—all but whoever's bandaging the skinned places on Joshu, that is. We never get home until five o'clock."

"Do you have to stay there all the time?" Mose asked.

"Where would I go?" Parri's eyes were honestly inquiring, and she said, "Sometimes I have one of the girls from Briarcliff with me and it isn't so bad. But they're usually so impressed by all the servants and things that they don't want to go back to my house. They'd rather just sit around. They aren't much fun."

"Most of them aren't," he agreed, "but I know some really sharp girls over there. Still, the high school crowd's better."

137

"I'm glad I'm going there."

They were silent, each thinking of the future, until Mose said, "What about Sunday?"

"Why, I just told you," Parri answered, surprised. "Weren't you listening?"

"Sure, but I meant tomorrow. Do you have any special plans for tomorrow?" he asked.

She shrugged in a bewildered way, so he went on, "A friend of mine, Jake McKloskey, has a model A, and we usually hack around on Sunday afternoon, picking up a gang as we go, girls too. How about it if we pick you up?"

"Would you? I mean . . ." Parri hesitated before she asked, incredulous, "Would you *want* to?" And at his nod, she exclaimed, "Well, my goodness! It seems so queer."

"What does?"

"Why, somebody asking me to go someplace. I didn't even know you yesterday, and here you are . . ." She stopped and looked directly at him. "Are you sure you aren't asking me because you pity me?" she wanted to know.

"With all *you've* got?" She did look forlorn, staring at him with eagerness mixed with doubt, so he tried to frame his answer in a way that would make her believe him. "I don't care how dull your previous Sundays have been," he said. "I'm inviting you to try one of mine. Maybe you'll like it and maybe you won't, but I do wish you'd try it."

"Then I'd love to."

Footsteps sounded on the stairway, and she added quickly, "I'm sure I can. I'll ask Mums and Daddy tonight, and I'm sure they'll be glad to have me take my long, sour face out of their way. And if I can't make them understand about it, Uncle Bobby will. He knows you. Oh, thank you, Mose! I'll be looking forward to tomorrow afternoon. Oh, isn't it *exciting?*"

She scarcely heard the talk going on around her about Ti Me's new name. She did remember to thank Susan for a wonderful time, to put her arms in the sleeves of the coat Bobby held for her; and when Mose walked to her front steps with her and said, "We'll stop by Gladstone for you about two," she remembered to say, "I'll be ready," and to add, "Good night."

The front door was still closing when she flung herself into the living room where her parents sat reading a play. "I'm *made!*" she cried, her arms outspread. "I'm going to meet a whole bunch of kids tomorrow—all at once!" Then she stumbled across the room and threw herself at her mother's feet. "Oh, Mums," she implored, hugging Penny's knees, "please pray they'll like me."

"Why, darling!" Penny leaned down and said, "Of course they will, whoever they are."

And at that Parri came to enough to sit up and tell about her glorious day that had begun unexpectedly at four o'clock. "It was simply super," she said at the end, "and Uncle Bobby's a doll. But I did do something awful," she confessed, her lifted eyes pleading for understanding. "I told Mose that I'm going to high school next year. I even *emphasized* it. He thinks I am."

"Well, so you are." Josh got up and sat on the arm of his wife's chair, right above Parri, so he could look down on her. "Not next year, though," he said. "Next term. We finally got to see the principal today."

"Daddy, you *didn't!* It can't be true!" Parri cried, rising to her knees. "But tell me it is."

"It is."

Parri and Josh answered together, and Parri reached up to hug them both. It was a lopsided oval of a hug because the recipients weren't on the same level, and it knocked them into each other, but Parri shed happy tears on them impartially.

"Oh, lucky, lucky me," she said; wiping her eyes on her father's necktie. "I'm so happy I could jump up and down, like April."

CHAPTER 9

"Where do you think you are going?" Davy asked as Parri skidded through the front hall, pulling on her coat as she went.

"Out," she answered, not stopping.

She had watched and waited for Mose, and hadn't allowed him to reach the front door. Once inside, she knew it would take ages to get him out again, because her mother and father, the uncles and aunts and cousins, even her grandparents, would want to look him over. "You just take him and run," Bobby had advised, finding her stationed at one of the long windows in the hall, her coat on a chair. Now here was Davy.

"Good-bye," she said, not wanting to waste a

precious second; and she jerked open the heavy door.

Mose was halfway across the wide, tiled terrace, and there were two boys and another girl waiting in the car. The girl also wore a camel's hair coat, Parri was thankful to see, and Mose had on gray flannel slacks under a plush-collared car coat, so she was dressed just right. "Hi," she said, as if she had always known him. "Let's hurry before Davy or somebody comes out." And they ran down the steps together.

"This is Jake," Mose said, pointing to the driver. "Jean Austen back there, and Park Talmadge. Want us both to sit up front with you, Jake?"

Parri couldn't believe that she was actually riding on the high front seat of a noisy old car between two boys. She was doing something the girl called Jean probably did every Sunday, and she leaned back with such a contented sigh that Mose grinned across at her.

"We thought we ought to do something special for you today," he said, "so we got together and cooked up this idea."

"What?" she asked eagerly.

"You wait and see. You may not like it, but it was the best we could do on short notice."

"I'll like *anything!*" Parri twisted around to look at the two on the back seat. "I guess you've never seen anyone as excited as I am," she said.

"But Mose probably told you I would be." The girl called Jean looked pretty and pleasant; so Parri smiled especially at her. "I thought I never could wait for two o'clock to come," she said, sliding back into place again.

No one quite understood it, but they all believed her. How, they had wondered, could anyone who had so much—money, an actress for a mother, rich relatives—be as left out of things as Mose had said Parri was? Then Mose had explained it; and out of curiosity, if nothing else, they had agreed to give her a big day. The girls were skeptical, the boys wary. Penny Parrish was a famous name around town, and what would her daughter be like? But everyone Mose had telephoned had agreed to show up at his house.

"Why, we're going to West Point," Parri said, recognizing a familiar road that went in the opposite direction from town.

"Yep," Mose answered, still managing to be mysterious. "Wouldn't you like a tour around?"

"Why, yes." Parri had toured all over the place only a week ago, with April, but she was glad to do it again. It had been pretend with April; now it was real. "I'd love it," she said, as they went through the gates and past the hotel where she and April had sat and planned what they would wear to an imaginary dance. They had chosen satin and chiffon. Now here she was in a brown wool pleated skirt and a tan sweater.

They passed the quadrangle, Grant Hall, the parade ground; then the car turned to wind up a hill where the officers' quarters were. "My goodness, I haven't been up here since I was little," she said, looking. "One of Uncle David's classmates was stationed here, and he and Mums brought the whole bunch of us up. My grandparents used to live in one of the houses, but I don't remember which one."

"This is it," Mose said, as the car drove around a circle and stoppped before a square, red-brick house that had a sunroom on one end. "Your Uncle Bobby told me so. *We* live in it now."

"Well, this *is* a surprise." Parri leaned forward and tried to picture her mother running in and out of the house; her Uncle David, too; and cadets, as her mother had said they had; and even the two noisy little Parrishes who had grown up to be her Uncle Bobby and Aunt Tippy. But the others had shoved open the car's stubborn doors and were getting out. "Are we going inside?" she asked, pleased. "Oh, good!"

"Come on." Mose wondered why she hadn't noticed several other cars parked at the curb and in the driveway, but he waited while she stood looking at the house, forgetful of the others. Then she gave a little skip. "Oh, this is exciting," she said. "I feel just like Alice in Wonderland. And do you know," she said to Jean, who had lived all her life in the house her great-grandparents had built, "I bet I'll know exactly where the coat closet is. Aunt Tippy got locked in there once when she was little, and they were ages finding her. And if I get to go upstairs," she whispered, "I'll know which room belonged to Mums. It's on the southwest corner."

Jean began to like this strange girl Mose had thrust into their close-knit gang. Parri didn't know she was enlarging it by one, that she belonged neither to the army group nor the one in town. She didn't know anything from anything, Jean decided, but she was really cute. So she made herself Parri's personal sponsor. She walked beside her along the cement walk, that was only wide enough for two, and let Mose be first up the steps to a small portico.

"This is Parri, gang," Mose shouted, flinging open the door. "Parri, this is the gang."

Parri stood in the middle of a small hall and stared. She shook with excitement and her hands trembled. "Well—oh—h-hello," she stammered, listening to fifteen names but hearing none of them. And then some silly tears pushed against her eyes. From a starvation diet to a banquet was too much and too quick. "Oh, my goodness," she said, and put her hand over her quivering mouth.

They liked her. Somehow she knew they did, because they were all so kind. They toured her over the house and laughed when she told about the things her mother had done, and whooped when she described how her Uncle Bobby had put a burr in the chair of an officer who later became President of the United States. It didn't occur to her that they liked her because she had almost cried. Had she been important and haughty, as they had expected her to be, they would have patiently sat through an hour of her, then made excuses to leave.

"I just can't believe I'm me," she said, sitting on the floor in the smallish sunroom, just as her mother must have done hundreds of times, with a snub-nosed girl and two high school juniors of the football team surrounding her. "Last week I couldn't get anybody to come to a party I wanted to give, and now look at me!"

There were moments when she felt as if she were Penny Parrish, especially when Mose's brother, who was a cadet, came in with his parents. Why, he could be Uncle David, she thought, and they could be Grandpa and Grandma; and she sprang up to speak to them.

But gradually it all began to straighten out. She became Parrish MacDonald when she helped the girls unpack their picnic baskets, and she was a sputtering, incoherent Parri when she telephoned home and told her parents where she was.

"They're just as pleased as I am," she said to Mose, waiting outside the door of the sunroom for her. "They couldn't believe it."

Mose knew they could, because his boss had been instructed to tell them. They had known where she was going and when to expect her home, long before she had left them. But they had been as good at keeping the secret as he.

"Who's that cute blond girl?" Parri asked, as they went back to the kitchen. "I think Jean's darling, but I'm trying to sort them out. Jean's a sophomore, but the one with light hair will be in my class." And then, before he could answer, she stopped and clutched his arm. "I'm going to high school *next term*," she confided breathlessly. "Isn't it super? I am, and that's why it's so important to know who is who."

"You'll have plenty of time," he answered. "You don't think this is the last time you'll be with us before then, do you?"

"Do you mean things like this happen often?" she asked.

"Not exactly like this," he answered, "because we're pretty much separated during the week. The town crowd pals around together, and so does the post crowd. We get together a lot, though; and if there's something special going on at school, we stay in for it and catch a later bus. We'll see that you get home," he added, seeing her face cloud with doubt.

"Then it's all right. I'll get to know everyone as fast as I can." And she hurried out to serve plates, wash pans, and do whatever else needed to be done. She was like a kitten with a catnip mouse. Exhilarated. Stimulated. And when they all trooped down to a basement room with their plates and mugs of cocoa, she thought it was the most beautiful basement she had ever seen.

It wasn't at all like her pine-paneled basement room at home, because army quarters belong to the government, and their occupants aren't permitted to remodel or decorate them. This one had whitewashed walls and a cement floor; but an old rattan screen had been set before some shelves that held all the leftovers a family couldn't bear to throw away, yet seldom used. There were army cots heaped with bright pillows against the four walls, and rattan chairs from Hong Kong were scattered about, with tin tables beside them. There was a card table with four wobbly dining-room chairs in one corner, and in another a large electric heater blew out great gusts of hot air.

Parri found herself on one of the army cots, between the blond girl whose name was Barbie Andrews and a snub-nosed boy whom everyone called Dicky-Wicky. He was Dick Wicks, she learned later, and a clowning favorite. The cot sagged, so it was hard to reach forward to one of the three brightly painted nail kegs before them for sips of cocoa; and since Dicky-Wicky was always hopping up and down, forks clattered on the cement and buttered rolls skittered off into space. The rolls weren't very clean, either, after Dicky-Wicky had finished juggling them and redistributing them, but Parri didn't care. She got one with a bite out of it and thought it delicious.

Nobody had asked her about her mother and father—not once. Usually they did. Almost every girl at school had cornered her at some time or other and said something like, "I saw your mother in her last play—you know, the one your father produced and directed for her. I thought she was perfectly wonderful, and they do make the most fascinating team. Tell me, are they really as much in love as the magazine articles say they are?"

"Yes," Parri would reply sparingly, tight inside.

This crowd didn't care. The army half was interested in the anecdotes she had told about another army family who had lived in this house, and the town half kept giving her the names of boys in the country who drove their own cars to school and suggesting she get in a car pool. Bobby had primed Mose, and Mose had passed on the word, but she didn't know it. She was grateful only for being accepted as herself.

"I can't wait for February," she said to Barbie, during one of the times when Dicky-Wicky was out in the middle of the room, doing a trick with a deck of cards he had found. "I know I'm a kook, but do you suppose everybody would come . . ." Something stopped her. "Don't rush things," a small voice whispered. "Don't lose these friends the way you lost April. Play it safe, so you won't get hurt again." "I'm just a kook," she said helplessly.

"No, you aren't." Barbie set her plate on her nail keg, then leaned back and said, "I haven't been here so long myself, and at first I was just as eager as you are. My dad couldn't take the city, so he opened a law practice out here. We like it, and I wouldn't go back for the world."

"But we've lived here forever," Parri said. "We're practically natives, yet I don't know a soul."

"You will." Barbie answered, as if she understood what Parri had been about to say by promising, "It won't be long until you'll have this whole gang and maybe more in your house. I know you can't see much of the school until you really start going there, but how would you like to come in on the bus tomorrow and let me show you around? We can have supper afterward at my house, and Dad and I'll drive you home."

"Tomorrow?" Another date so soon? Supper with another girl on a weekday night? Parri was overcome. "Oh, mercy," she said, "I'd love it! I'll come straight to the high school as fast as I can." And then she looked up and saw Mose.

"How's it going?" he asked, having left a pouting black-haired girl named Natalie to come over and look after his protégée. Whenever he got paired off—which wasn't often because of his studies and his job—it was with Natalie Parker. She had resented his interest in Parri and was giving him a hard time, so he only listened to Parri say, "Just fine," and hustled off to turn on the record player.

"He's really something from outer space," Parri said. Then she saw Barbie watching Mose and frowning. "Did I say something wrong?" she asked anxiously.

"No." Barbie took a deep breath, clamped her lips together, then exploded, "Darn Natalie!" And that was all Parri could get her to say. Dicky-Wicky came back with Jake; and before Parri quite realized it, the whole party became general again. Dishes were washed, the basement room left clean, and those with homework to do began to leave.

"I'd like to tell your mother and father goodbye," Parri said, when she and Jake and Jean were the only ones left and Mose was bringing out a pile of coats.

"They went to a supper party at the club," Mose answered, letting Jake and Jean help themselves, then holding Parri's. "They're used to this and don't expect any thanks, poor souls. When my little sister grows up, they'll really get it."

151

Parri thought he hustled them all out to the car. She even thought Jake drove too slowly to suit him because he was silent while they chattered around him. But when he walked up her front steps with her, he seemed relaxed again and like himself.

"If there's a bust after the basketball game Saturday night I'll let you know," he said. "There may be, because it's our first practice game. We'll come by and get you. Okay?"

"Oh, thank you!" Stars shone in Parri's eyes as she said, "I owe you so much, Mose! You've done so much for me that I can't ever tell you how grateful I am. Why, you've turned my whole life upside down. It's like suddenly tipping over the world," she said. "Instead of starving in China—whoops, the world rolls over and you're eating steak in Paris. It's just like that."

"I'm glad. Good night, Parri." Mose gave her shoulder a pat and went back to the car. Natalie didn't believe he had done all this for his boss's niece. She had at first, but not after she saw Parri. He didn't quite believe it himself.

Parri stood watching the car drive away. She was still excited and happy. Natalie Parker had been only one of eighteen faces; and knowing nothing of her jealousy, Parri tried to single out the ones she liked best. There was Mose, of course. And Jake and Jean and Barbie. She liked Jake because he looked and acted like a cowboy, and Jean because she was really sweet and kind. She liked the silly Dicky-Wicky too, and a tall thin boy named Alan something-or-other who had put on an apron and helped her wash the dishes. But she liked Barbie best of all the girls. There was something about Barbie that reminded her of April, in a more wholesome way.

"Hoo-hoo," she called, opening the door and going in. "Here comes your popular daughter." And as she pulled off her coat she added gratefully, "Thanks to your brother Bobby!"

CHAPTER 10

IT WAS A RAW DAY, with a hint of snow in the air. Davy had ridden in the morning because he had no classes, and by midafternoon was so tired of reading and wandering restlessly about the house that he wished he had gone to college with his friends.

Why keep on hoping for West Point? he asked himself. A Congressman friend of his father's had already wasted two appointments on him, finally giving them to his alternates; the Superintendent of the Academy, a friend of his grandfather's, had called him in and suggested—even urged—that he try some other career.

"The army isn't everything," the General had said. "Later in life you'll learn that."

And Davy had answered dutifully, "Yes, sir," when he wanted to say, "It's all very fine for you to advise me. You *got* your appointment." Not even the assurance that he would have been a credit to the service had made up for the discouragement he had felt when he came out. The Supe, he thought unhappily, didn't want Uncle Sam to take a chance on me.

"I'm going out, Mom," he called up the stairway. "Be back for dinner." Then he put his riding coat on over his heavy pull-over sweater and went out to his car.

It was while he was aimlessly starting the motor that he remembered Parri. Parri had a big-brother image of him, and so, with nothing better to do, he might as well go over and see how she was coming along. There were no cars in either the driveway or the garage when he pulled up at the side of the MacDonalds; but as he was getting out of his car, a station wagon came swoooping in and stopped behind him.

"Hi," his Aunt Penny called, running down her window and leaning out. "What brings you over?"

"I thought I'd see how Parri's doing," he answered, walking back to her. "Is she around?"

"Parri? Mercy, no." She leaned over to open the door and said, "Get in. I have to pick up Minna and go back to town," she explained, when he was beside her and she had closed everything up again, "but let's talk a minute. For you to ask if

Parri's around makes me laugh. I never see her."

"Why not?"

"She has friends." Penny ran her gloved hands along the wheel and said, "I'm not sure I like it. I used to feel awfully sorry for her when she was continually following me around like a lost kitten, but now I only see her when I'm taking her somewhere. Barbie spent last weekend out here, and Parri's spending this one with Barbie. I just took her clothes in."

"So what?" Davy grinned at her and stretched his booted legs out. "It's exactly what you did at her age, isn't it?"

"Yes—no." Penny considered the question before she answered it. "We all lived in a bunch at Fort Arden. I never went very far away from home."

"You went to school in town, and sometimes the town kids gave dances at their country club—I've heard Dad say so. You weren't always hooked to Grandma and Grandpa."

"No, I guess I wasn't. Oh, darn." Penny turned her head to look at Davy, wishing he belonged to her. She wanted him to be another David, taking Parri wherever she went. She even wished Joshu could grow older faster and pass Parri. Poor little thing, he couldn't. That made her smile, so she settled down to tell Davy in more detail about Parri's social life. "If I take time out," she asked, when it was growing cold in the car, "will you come in and drink a Coke while I have tea?"

"No, thanks." He was already opening the door, but he reached back and patted her knee. "Stop worrying," he said, sliding out, "or you'll get gray hairs. I'll talk to the kid when I see her and steady her down."

"Oh, will you?" Penny didn't know what on earth Davy could say to Parri, because she was only behaving in a normal way. Every girl needs friends, she knew and she liked all of Parri's. "Oh, let it go," she said crossly. "Let's not spoil her fun."

"I don't intend to." Davy grinned at her. "Take it easy," he said, leaning in. Then he closed the door and went back to his own car that had stayed warm with its motor running.

Now where to go, he wondered, backing out after the station wagon that wove a crazy path until it charged off into the front driveway. Bitsy's? She might be home or she might be at her cozy little bookshop. He decided to try her house first.

She was there, and she welcomed him. "You're just the man I want to see!" she cried, rushing to answer his ring. She looked like an Eskimo, in a woolly car coat with a hood and fur-lined boots. "Ellin just told me I have to take a cake and some cookies to Vance, because he can't get home this weekend; and the heater's broken in Dad's car, so he took mine and left me his. You'll drive me to Grant Hall, won't you?"

"Sure. Come on."

It was good to be needed somewhere, so he set her basket in the car and watched her slide gratefully in beside it and push back her hood. "Whew," she said, "I'm frightfully hot. I didn't look forward to playing Little Red Ridinghood in a cold car. I'd rather ride with the wolf."

"Grrrrr," Davy snarled, baring his teeth. "I feel about as wolfish today as an oyster."

"What's wrong?" Bitsy rested her elbow on the basket and leaned toward him. "You didn't hear bad news about your physical, did you?"

"Nope. It's still coming up in April, but I have a hunch I won't be among the candidates to be examined," he answered. And as they drove along he told her what the Superintendent of the Military Academy had tried to make clear.

"That's not fair!" Bitsy declared hotly when he had finished. "It's not up to him to discourage you. You know what you can do, and so do I. You can march as far and as long as the others, and you can leap over whatever they have to leap over, and even make a parachute jump if you have to."

"They don't jump at the Point," he told her, smiling at her ignorance.

"Well, they do go hopping around, and they

climb hills and carry little machine guns that they point at each other. I know that much because Neal told me. And Vance said he was going off to some crazy place today, so I was to leave his boodle with the guard in Grant Hall. You can do all that."

"I think so." Davy drove along, enjoying her indignation. "The Supe was only trying to cushion the blow," he said when she waxed eloquent again. "He knows I can't make it, so he was only trying to keep me from trying."

"You can so, Davy Parrish, you *can!* I wish I could get up in front of that medical board and tell them a thing or two. I'd say to them. . . ." They were approaching the quadrangle of barracks, and she broke off to cry, "My word! What's going on?"

Three canvas-topped army trucks stood in a row, and the street was swarming with cadets wearing their fatigue uniforms under heavy padded coats. Cadet officers were calling out names, and several regular officers were moving about.

"Looks like a special exercise," Davy answered, stopping to ask a cadet sergeant if it was all right to go through.

"No, hold it," the cadet said, "until the trucks move out. Some plebe got himself lost, and we're sending out a search party. It won't be but a few minutes till we're out of your way."

159

"It wasn't Vance Jordon, was it?" Davy asked through the open window, feeling Bitsy leaning across him.

"No, I just saw him around somewhere. It was Dedrick, or Deeping, or—Deering, that's it, Mark Deering."

"How come?" Davy asked, as Bitsy moved back with a sigh of relief.

"I don't know. One of his roommates just missed him. There was a mapping problem on B hill, and the sergeant in charge said he counted off afterward, but . . . Hey, mister," he shouted, advancing on a bewildered fourth classman who was trying to climb into a truck that was already filled. "Get back in line." Then he turned to Davy again and grinned. "I'm sure glad I'm not the sergeant who goofed," he said. "You can go on through now."

But Davy swung the car around in a U turn and headed back toward home.

"Hey, what about my boodle?" Bitsy asked, but he shook his head.

"Forget about the boodle," he said. "I'm going out there. I know every foot of the terrain they use for problems better than anyone around here. I can get up and down those rocky hills on Sing better and faster than the guys on foot, and I don't have to follow a road like the trucks."

"But it's getting dark," she protested.

"What of it? Sing and I've been out in the dark before."

Bitsy thought he drove too fast, but she held on and kept silent because she knew he was planning what he would do. And after he had swung into a lane that led straight to Gladstone's stables, he said, "You drive the car on up to the house and tell the folks where I've gone. We'll take the boodle over to Vance when I get back."

"It doesn't matter." Bitsy braced herself for a sudden stop, and said as he threw open the door and jumped out, "Just you be careful!"

"I will."

It was already deep gloom inside the stable, and Singing Star, waiting for his supper of hay and oats, looked over the top of his box stall and gave a soft whinny. But it wasn't one of the stable hands who flicked on the lights. Davy said, "Hi, fellow," and slipped a bridle over the surprised horse's head. "We've got work to do," he went on, leading Singing Star up the aisle and tying him to a ring in a post. Then he dived into the tack room and came back with a saddle. "At ease, boy," he said, fastening the girth and disappearing again. He found a flashlight on a shelf and put it in one pocket; a first-aid kit went into the other, followed by a roll of linen bandage. Then he took a trench coat from a hook and put it on, and snatched a clean horse blanket from a tack box. It was all done with economy of

161

motion, and he rolled the blanket and strapped it to the cantle of the saddle before he swung himself astride Singing Star's back.

"Move out, old boy," he said, gently kicking the reluctant horse's sides and starting him off at a trot.

They were galloping smoothly when they crossed the graveled lane and went over a low fence into pasture land; and long before they reached the end of Gladstone's grazing acres, Davy could see the lights of the trucks in the distance. He thought of changing course and going over past them, but they were too far to his right and parked a long way from B hill.

It was quite dark now; and far away, like twinkling fireflies, he could see smaller lights flashing. They meant that the men were still searching, so he took Singing Star over another fence and eased him down for the rough way to come.

All during the time when he had been driving home and saddling up, he had tried to figure out what someone who was lost out there would do. It had been still daylight when the cadet had become separated from his squad; but with no sun to steer by, which way would he go? Davy thought he knew. There were many deceptive paths through those hills, and one seemingly easy and logical one led straight into a dead-end canyon. Davy had taken it once by mistake, so someone else could—someone on foot, perhaps, who wouldn't know how to find his way out.

"Take it easy, Sing," he said to his horse, circling the wavering lights and plunging into a cavern of blackness.

Loose rocks clattered and spilled off into space as Davy followed a narrow path that was halfway up a hillside. It curved in an arc around the hill and was leading him far away from the other searchers, but it would bring him to a spot that would take them an hour or more to reach—if they knew where they were going, which he doubted.

"Okay. Down we go," he said five minutes later, pulling Singing Star to a stop, then swinging him straight at what appeared to be a deep black pit. "Easy does it. You've taken this slide before, boy. Get set."

Singing Star's forefeet went over the rim, and he tucked his haunches under him. More rock clattered like hail, and Davy, lying almost flat along his horse's back, could feel cold wind bite at his face as they slid straight down.

"Good boy," he said, when they landed and Sing jumped over the icy bed of a stream. "You —darned—good—boy."

He gave the horse a pat, then reached under his trench coat for his flashlight. They were in the treacherous canyon now, so he used both his light and his voice.

"Hey, Deering!" he shouted, flashing his light about. "Hey, there! *Deering!*" Only silence answered him as he had expected, so he pushed on and kept calling.

"Mark! Mark Deering!" Still silence. A small startled animal rustled off into the dead, dried leaves; twigs snapped like popguns from the broken branches under Singing Star's feet, but there was no other sound to break the vast stillness. Then the hint of path Davy followed branched off in a Y, and he stopped to consider.

The right-hand fork was the one he had already decided his cadet would be following. It was broken in the middle by a deep gully that had been the rocky bed of an old stream, but Deering couldn't know that. It looked good from the other side and as if it might lead somewhere. "Here we go again," he said, and turned Sing to the right.

He didn't know what he expected to find when he reached the gully, because only a Hercules of a man could swing himself up onto the ledge of rock from which Sing would have to jump down. Certainly no tired cadet could make it. If Mark Deering had gotten that far, he had either stopped or turned back.

"*Helloool!*" he called, reining in at the top of the ledge. "Hell*oooo*, Mark! Mark Deering! Are you down there?" He thought he heard a moan, but couldn't be sure, so called again. "Mark? Are you there?" he shouted, swinging his light about.

"I'm—here," a weak voice answered. "Help—me."

"Coming." Davy knew Singing Star could leap from the ledge. They had done it once in daylight, so he crouched far over the horse's neck this time and held his flashlight on the landing place. It was no time to spot Deering, he knew, not until they were safely down. "Let's go," he said.

Singing Star landed like a cat, but even so Davy's head snapped from the sudden stop. The flashlight was clamped in his numb fingers that gripped the reins, and he raised it and swung it about in the blackness.

"Here," the voice answered weakly again, and Davy could see a dim form beyond the scrub pines.

Mark Deering was lying in a heap below the opposite cliff. He had lost his fatigue cap, and his matted black hair hung over dark eyes that were glazed with pain. He looked like a bundle of old clothes as Davy dismounted and bent over him, but he raised his head to say, "I think I passed out. Your voice must have brought me to. I kept hearing it and hearing it before I could answer, and then . . ."

"Just relax, you're all right now," Davy said. "I'm David Parrish. Wait till I tie my horse and I'll have a look at you."

"I think . . ." Mark Deering answered in a

quavering voice, when Davy had looped Singing Star's reins around the branch of a tree and come back, ". . . I think . . ." Then he shook his head to try to clear it. "I think I broke my wrist when I fell. I started to jump down, then—whambo. I guess I slipped on some ice. Do you think my wrist's broken?"

"Sorry, but it is." Davy didn't have to look very closely into the beam of his flashlight to see a bulge of bone pressing against Mark's skin. He wouldn't have pulled the wrist back into place had he known how, not until X rays had been taken, so he simply asked an important question. "Did you hit your head when you fell?"

"I don't think so. I might have, but I don't think so. I started to get up after I fell, and that's when I passed out. I rested my weight on my hands, and that's the last I remember."

Davy sat down and considered the situation. He could do one of two things. He could keep Mark warm under the horse blanket and build a fire to attract attention, then wait for the search party to see the glow and work its way to them; or he could load Mark on Sing and start back. A fire might set the whole scrubby woods ablaze, and was dangerous. If Mark had no concussion, a ride on a horse wouldn't hurt him. Which to do? The only way was to ask his patient.

"Listen," he said, trying to be brusque instead of sympathetic while they made up their minds together, "I can't do much for you out here. I can make a sling for your arm out of a bandage I have, and wrap you up in a horse blanket I brought, but that's about all. The corps has search parties out, and one of 'em's sure to find us after a while. We can sit it out if you want to, or we can go meet them."

"Let's go." Mark's thoughts were clearer now, and he managed to pull himself to a sitting position by using his good hand. And even though he winced with pain, he took a deep breath and asked, "How did you get here?"

"I heard the news, so I rode out," Davy answered. "I live around here."

"Lucky for me. Let's go."

He would have struggled to his feet, but Davy held him down. "We have to be sure you didn't hit your head," he said, seeing dried leaves in Mark's thick brush of hair. "It's no good taking a chance."

"I didn't hit my head, I'm sure." Mark tapped his forehead to prove it. "Nothing hurts. No headache, no bruise," he said, feeling carefully. Then he groaned again as his body moved a little.

"Okay. I'll make a sling." Davy took the roll of bandage from his pocket and carefully lifted Mark's arm into a comfortable position. His fingers were stiff and had no feeling in them, but he managed it. The he put the blanket around Mark and stood up to look back toward civilization.

No flashlights dotted the night. Spotlights from the trucks wove crisscross arcs above the trees, but they were far away and provided only a distant beacon, like that of a lighthouse guiding a storm-tossed ship on a straight course across the sea. There could be no straight course here. Too many hills and gullies lay between this lonesome spot and the lights.

"I guess we might as well try it," he said, wishing he had brought something hot for them to drink—soup, preferably, since it was long past six o'clock. "You'll have to hold your wrist against you while I boost you up on Sing."

"How are you going to get wherever we're going?" Mark asked, when after a minimum of pain he was in the saddle and wrapped in the horse blanket.

"Walk." Davy held Singing Star close to his bit and flashed the light in front of them. "If we go along this valley for a little way, I know a dip in the cliff where we can get up on higher ground without jerking you too much. Somebody may see us from there."

"They never would have found me down here," Mark groaned, trying not to faint again from shock, cold, and pain. His ribs hurt even more than his wrist, and while nothing would have made him tell Davy so, he was sure he had broken some of them, too, in his fall.

"How did you happen to get separated from the others?" Davy asked, having noticed the way Mark held to the low pommel of the English saddle with his good hand and sat bent sidewise, but deciding that sympathy would do no good and conversation might.

"Darned if I know. The sergeant told Coulter and me to go down and map the second ridge, and we did. One minute Coulter was there and the next he wasn't. I like mapping, so I suppose I just got interested and didn't hear the whistle. Maybe I walked too far away to get a better view of something or maybe I just didn't hear Coulter leave. Anyway, when I found I was out there by myself, I started back."

"So you thought." Davy looked up to grin, even though Mark Deering was only a blurred shape above him in the dark; then he looked ahead at the break in the trees his flashlight beam was searching for and said, "We'll get back on the beaten track now."

"I'll bet they never would have found me down where I was," Mark repeated gratefully. "Not until morning, anyway, and I'd have been frozen solid by then. Where do you say you live?"

"Over yonder." Davy swept his flashlight around vaguely, then directed it back to the low but steeply rising bank. "Sing's going to have to rough you up a little when he makes the climb," he said. "Try not to jerk if you can help it, and you'll be all right. Hold on and press your heels down in the stirrups to steady yourself. Ready?"

"Uh—yeah."

Mark squinted his eyes shut and gritted his teeth as Davy scrambled up the slippery, icy hill and pulled Singing Star behind him. He was breathing harder than Davy when they reached the top, but he managed to praise, "Gosh, you must be some athlete to charge up that and haul a horse behind you."

"Oh, I am." Davy disgustedly compared himself with this cadet he was bringing in. Mark Deering had been found physically fit to withstand four years in the United States Military Academy, while he had been branded a cripple. But aloud he said, "If we keep left, we ought to run into your buddies."

"Who would like to cut my throat."

The way was easier now, and Davy let out the reins and walked in front of Singing Star. He kept lifting his light to flash it above the trees, and every now and then he would call "Hellooo. Helloool" And after what seemed hours and hours to Mark, who had seen nothing but strange lights crisscrossing the sky, he said, "The trucks are behind that next hill. It won't be long now."

Mark's eyes were closed, and Davy was holding him in the saddle when they came into a clearing and out to the narrow road where the trucks waited. Two officers and a corporal saw them coming and ran forward.

"Where did you find him?" one of the officers asked; and Davy made a motion behind him.

"Back there," he said. "He's got a broken wrist, and from the way he grunts when he breathes, I'd say a couple of busted ribs. He's cold, too, so you'd better get him back to the hospital as fast as you can. You can keep the blanket."

"Thanks."

The two officers, one of them a doctor, lifted Mark from the saddle. Carefully, slowly, as if he might break somewhere else, they carried him to the truck and stretched him out on one of its long benches. They took his pulse and listened to his heart. They examined his wrist and felt his ribs, and when he asked through the pain, "Where'd he go? I want to thank him," they remembered Davy.

One climbed down, suddenly conscious that the horns on the trucks were blasting away, and looked about. There was no horse, no rider. "Where did the fellow go who brought Deering in?" he shouted up to one of the drivers.

"I don't know." The noise on that truck stopped, and the driver leaned out to yell above the din of the others, "He just said, 'Blow your horns and make all the racket you can,' and he got on his horse and rode off."

"Which way?"

"Search me."

The lone rescuer, whoever he was, was gone. The officer took off his cap and stood for some seconds scratching his head in a puzzled way. There was nothing but ebony black around him, and he thought of having the searchlights turned down to sweep it. But what good would it do? Whoever was out there would be far away by now. And besides, he had a duty to perform, he told himself. He had a patient to deliver to the hospital. After that, with luck and good fortune, he could get home in time to take his wife to the movies.

CHAPTER 11

"Where do you think Davy could be?" Bitsy asked, unable to remain as still as the others in the drawing room at Gladstone.

She marveled at Davy's mother, who was knitting furiously, as if the sweater she was making for Carli must be finished in a few minutes; and at his grandmother, sitting with her hands folded idly in her lap. She could not know that Carrol was dropping stitches without knowing it, and that Mrs. Parrish's knuckles were white between her tightly laced fingers.

Only Penny was pacing restlessly about, picking up china ornaments and putting them down without looking at them. Every now and then she stopped before the three men who were sitting in a group around the fire, and now she said, as if in answer to Bitsy's question, "It's almost ten o'clock, David. Can't you *do* something?"

"What would you suggest?" He looked up at her and said quietly, "Davy went off on a mission. When he's finished it he'll come home. That's all I can say, Pen. Except to remind you that there are also dozens of cadets out there. He's not alone."

"But they should have found the silly boy by now and come back."

The MacDonalds and Colonel and Mrs. Parrish had driven over after dinner, as soon as they had heard the news. Not because they were worried about Davy then, but to hear his own account of an exciting adventure.

"Davy went off to help find some lost cadet," Carol had related in her customary evening telephone chat with Penny. "He'd had Bitsy with him, and he dumped her at the stable and went off on his horse. She left the car there for him and walked up, so we kept her here for dinner. Oh, of course he's all right, Pen," she had said in answer to a question from Penny, but looking anxiously at her watch that said twenty minutes to eight. "He'll be here any second, but come on over if you want to." So here they all were, waiting.

"I don't see how they could go running around hunting for a boy until ten o'clock," Penny said,

174

going to join Bitsy at one of the long back windows that showed the brightly lighted stable in the distance and the dark shape of Davy's car before it. "I don't think it's good for Davy to overdo."

"Davy's strong," her father reminded. "There's nothing wrong with him."

"Oh, you know there is. He . . ." She broke off because something in David's face stopped her. His mouth was tight, and a muscle twitched along his jaw. And just then the telephone rang. "I'll get it," she said thankfully, rushing off to the library before anyone else could move.

"Hello," she said, hoping to hear Davy's voice; but Parri's came back to her, crackling with excitement.

"Minna told me where you were," Parri cried. "Oh, isn't it exciting? Aren't you all proud of Davy? Aren't you simply bursting?"

"Why, yes." Penny wondered how Parri, far away in town, could know about Davy, when his own parents here at home had no idea where he was. But Parri was rattling on:

"Mose called us up and told us all about it. His brother told the family—he's a first classman, you know—and he said everybody in his barracks is simply buzzing over it! And just think," she cried, "it was Vance Jordon who figured out who Davy was! Isn't that something?"

"How—how did Vance know?" Penny asked,

probing for information by asking a question that seemed safe.

"Why, after Davy had brought the cadet back to the trucks, all smashed up and riding Sing while Davy walked, he just disappeared. Somebody wanted to thank him, but he wasn't there. Didn't you know that?"

"No," Penny said.

"Well, he wasn't. And after the rest of the dumb rescuers got back to barracks, they began to tell about it. Vance heard them and asked some questions, and right away he knew. He told the tac—he's a tactical officer," Parri explained, having had Mose enlighten her, "and the tac called the hospital, and sure enough the busted-up cadet remembered hearing Davy said 'David.' Davy doesn't much like being called Davy," Parri said. "Did you know that?"

"No," Penny said again. And she asked. "What time was all this?"

"Oh, I don't know. It was after nine o'clock before they found out about Davy, I guess, because the dumb part of the search party had already been to mess hall and come back to barracks. Could I talk to Davy a minute?"

"He isn't here right now, dear."

"He isn't? Where'd he go?"

"Just—out for a little while." Penny wanted to end the conversation quickly. They really had something to worry about now, she thought, trying to figure time while she listened to Parri's voice. If the squads had finished eating and gone back to barracks at nine o'clock, it meant that at eight, or even seven-thirty . . . "What did you say, dear?" she asked.

"I said that Davy's probably gone over to Bitsy's to tell her all about it, and that Barbie and I are coming home early in the morning and are going to spend the weekend at my house. There'll probably be a terrific amount of excitement, and we don't want to miss any of it. It isn't often you get a cousin who's a hero. Mums?"

"Yes, honey?"

"Davy's . . ." Parri's voice was hesitant as it said, "You sound so funny. You don't sound excited. Davy's all right, isn't he? He isn't too tired, or sick, or anything, is he?"

"Of course not, darling. But he's so shy, you know." Penny tried to make her explanation sound reasonable, and she added, "We didn't know half of what you've told us. We're grateful."

"Oh, swell. I'll let you know if I hear anything more," Parri said proudly, convinced and satisfied. "I probably will, and anyway I'll be home in the morning. Oh, Mums," she cried, "isn't it terrific?"

"It is indeed." Penny wanted to hang up. The others were waiting to learn as much, or as little, as she had. But Parri was still talking.

"I bet he won't have any trouble getting into West Point now," she was saying. "I bet they'll simply *beg* him to come there. And they'll probably give him a medal or something. Mose's brother's sure they'll give a review for him. And, Mums, maybe the President of the United States will pin a medal on him. Oh, gosh!"

"I hope so. Good night, honey, I have to go now." Penny couldn't wait a second longer. She would call Parri back when Davy was found, she decided, so dropped the receiver into its cradle and hurried back to the drawing room.

"That was Parri," she said, and as quietly as she could, she told them. "It's been at least two hours," she ended, "since he rode away from the trucks."

Where was he? Everyone asked himself or herself that question. Had his leg given out? Had Singing Star thrown him? Was he lying out in the cold somewhere, as the hurt cadet had been? Then David stood up and took over.

"Let's keep our heads," he said calmly. "Davy's all right. He's an expert horseman. He's strong and able to take care of himself. I mean it," he said, putting his arm around his wife, who had come to him with a path of raveled knitting trailing behind her. "We've been waiting here believing that rescue operations were still going on. Well, they aren't. We know they aren't. They were over a long time ago."

"But where is Davy?" Carrol pleaded to know.

"Right where Lang would have looked, had he

been here. Where we should have known he'd be: tending his horse."

"But not all this time." Carrol shook her head and said, "It doesn't take two hours to groom a horse. I ride, so I know. And even if he's out in the stable," she reminded, "we have a telephone out there. He could have called us and told us what he's doing."

"Granted. He should have, but would he think to?" David rubbed her hair with his cheek and said, "I was a cadet when I was Davy's age. I didn't call home every time the corps made a move. I thought I was a man on my own. Davy does too."

"But, Mr. Parrish," Bitsy said, coming over, "he couldn't possibly be there. I've stayed right by the window all the time, and I've watched."

"You could have turned away for one minute and he could have ridden in," David said, smiling. Then he looked down at his wife. "Shall I be the one to break down and telephone him?" he asked.

"Yes." Carrol nodded. "But if he isn't there, I don't think I can bear it."

A door slammed somewhere far away, and footsteps whispered on the heavily padded carpet of a back hall. "Anybody home?" an unmistakable voice called. Then Davy appeared in the archway. He looked as freshly spruce as he had that morning, and he said in surprise, "Well, look who's here. Mom, you didn't tell me you were going to have the folks to dinner. Hi, Bitsy. Thanks for leaving the car."

"Oh, Davy!" His mother started toward him, then stopped. "We hear you're quite a hero," she said, as casually as she could.

"Oh, that." Davy grinned and shrugged. "The dumbjohn kid," he said. "He really banged himself up falling around in the dark, but he'll be all right. Sing will, too. He got a stone bruise somewhere along the line and went lame when I was almost home. I've been soaking his hoof and doctoring it. Mac came in on his rounds and made fresh coffee, but I'm darned hungry. How about coming with me, Bitsy, while I eat?" He started out, but turned around to ask, "What did you mean by saying you heard I'm a hero? Where'd you hear anything about it?"

"Parri telephoned," Penny said. "It's all over town that David Parrish was a one-man rescue party."

"Well, how do you like that? I thought I'd ridden off like the Lone Ranger used to when I was a kid, but I guess my mask slipped. Come on, Bits."

Those he left in the room watched to see if he limped. His boots that had been shined during his stay in the stable moved lightly, and he called back, "Hope you didn't worry too much about your baby boy."

"Oh, we didn't." Penny was the one who answered again, and she wanted to shake him. "But I'll tell you one thing," she shouted after him. "If Joshu ever goes off and lets Josh and me worry about where he is until after ten o'clock, I'll murder him!"

And at that Davy came back. "You weren't worried, were you, Mom?" he asked, taking his mother's face between his hands and looking anxiously into it.

"Not too much, dear," she said. "Your father wasn't worried, so I wasn't. I suppose I really wasn't a bit more anxious than I usually am when Lang goes tearing around the countryside in a car."

"Keep it that way." Davy rubbed his nose against hers and said, "Old Lang's a careful guy, and so'm I. Be back in a minute."

They watched him take Bitsy by the arm and march her off, and David was the first to comment, "He acts as if nothing has happened—as if it were all a part of his day. You know, I believe he honestly thinks it was."

"I do too, knowing Davy," Colonel Parrish returned. And he said to his wife, "We might as well go home, Marjorie. We'll get a lot more out of Parri tomorrow than out of this clam. Ready?"

"I'm ready," Mrs. Parrish agreed, getting up just as the doorbell rang.

"Now who could that be at this hour?" Carrol

181

asked wonderingly, when the bell sounded again. She started for the hall, then turned back to hide a smile as Perkins hurried to the door.

Perkins was struggling into his correct black jacket, but had on his flowered bedroom slippers, and she said behind her hand to David, "He must have been in a state over Davy to stay up this late when he didn't have to. Wait till he discovers what he has on his feet."

There were voices in the hall, a deep one and a softer high one, saying good evening to Perkins, so she and David went out to find the Superintendent of West Point and his wife standing uncertainly there.

"Why, General Claybourne, come in," David said, surprised almost into incoherence. "Well, Mrs. Claybourne, we haven't seen you for quite a while. Carrol, here are General and Mrs. Claybourne."

"We know we shouldn't have come so late," Mrs. Claybourne said, keeping her coat on but letting Carrol take her into the drawing room, "but Hubert thought we should."

"I'm so glad you did," Carrol answered. "Mums, Dad, here are the Claybournes. You know Penny and Josh," she added, secretly amused because Penny looked as if a flash bulb had gone off suddenly and caught her with her mouth open. "Please let me take your coats."

"No, no thanks." General Claybourne had managed to end his handshaking with the man to whom he often said he owed his career, Colonel Parrish. He had been a handsome young officer under Colonel Parrish's command, both before and during World War II, and the training he had had and the fine ideals he had been given to live up to had stayed with him, even after his superior officer had been wounded and forced to retire. That's a fine grandson you have, Dave," he said. "But he'd have to be if he belongs to you."

"Thanks, Hubert." Colonel Parrish stopped David as he went by, carrying Mrs. Claybourne's fur coat, after all. "Here's the fellow who's responsible for Davy," he said. "He and Carrol. Marjorie and I just sit back and watch the grandchildren grow."

"Then you've got something to watch. Tell me," the General asked David, "what do you think about your boy's performance tonight?"

"Well, sir," David's eyes twinkled as he answered, "if you knew my son better, you'd understand that we haven't heard much about it."

"You haven't?"

"No, sir. Nothing from Davy except, and I quote, 'The dumbjohn kid. He really banged himself up falling around in the dark, but he'll be all right.' Our voluble niece called us up and told us more than Davy did."

"Here, take my coat too." General Claybourne

pulled off his heavy civilian overcoat and handed it to David. "We just stopped by," he said to everyone, "on our way home from a dinner in town. The news reached me, there, and we took a chance on finding you up. We thought you'd be having a celebration."

"We would," Josh answered, not as awed by the military as Penny still was, "if we knew what to celebrate. You can't drink a toast to a horse that went lame."

"No reporters have called?"

"Should they have?" Mrs. Parrish asked.

"Oh, they will. The *Daily Chronicle* is always slow, and I suppose the cadets haven't flashed the news to New York yet. But they'll do it. One of them'll get through to Dad or Cousin Dick or Uncle Harry, and by morning your phone will start ringing. Anything that happens up here is fun for the press, and I'd squash this if it weren't for your boy's bravery. There's too much reported about delinquency nowadays to let an act of heroism go unnoticed."

"But Davy didn't do anything—dangerous, did he?" Carrol asked.

"No, I guess not." General Claybourne spoke lightly, but he contradicted the lightness by adding, "Unless you want to call it dangerous to go out in rugged country at night on a horse, taking chances I wouldn't have liked much, even in my young cavalry days. He was fine, and he accomplished what he set out to do—but that isn't what I came to talk to you about. He isn't around, is he?"

"He's having some supper," David said. "Shall I call him?"

"No, you're the ones I want to see. It's about your boy's future, so suppose we sit down while I tell you."

Only the men had been standing, so Josh nudged Penny farther along the sofa toward Mrs. Claybourne, Colonel Parrish chose the fireside bench, and David sat on the arm of Carrol's chair. It seemed suitable for General Claybourne to have the French antique that was upholstered in yellow brocade and looked a little like a throne.

"All fury's apt to break loose tomorrow," he said, when they were settled, "after the newspapers get hold of the thing. The Point will be accused of carelessness; parents will write in, the uproar will reach as far as Washington—but that will pass. The important thing is Davy. It is Davy, isn't it?" he looked around to ask.

"David," Penny answered, fresh from her conversation with Parri.

"David, then." He nodded as if trying to remember what he was about to say, then went on, "The important thing is what all this fuss is going to do to David. The corps will want to honor him with a review, which isn't bad in itself, since all he'd have to do would be to stand beside the Commandant and watch the companies go past him. It's an honor, as I said—but if it has to happen, I'm going to do my best to keep it simple."

"Thank you," Colonel Parrish said, knowing his grandson.

But David asked, "Why do you say 'if it has to happen,' sir?"

"Because I was wrong about the boy." General Claybourne shifted uneasily on his throne as he said soberly, "He came to see me, and I tried to discourage him from wanting to come to the Academy. I was honest with him—or so I thought—but after what he accomplished tonight, and after being told the names of four champion athletes who had polio when they were young, I'm sure I was wrong. I think David deserves the chance to prove he's physically fit, and personally I'm going to see that he gets it."

"Thank you very much, sir," David said.

"But just suppose he does get in," the General went on. "What's all this hullabaloo going to do to him? We can't keep the newspapers out, but stop and think what having had a review given in his honor will do to a plebe? This year's second classmen will be high-minded, top-ranking first classmen next year, and they'll take united pleasure in dishing out discipline to Mr. Importance Parrish for his own good. The plebes, having taken a lot of punishment themselves this year, will be only too happy to pile on, as yearlings."

"I see what you mean," David answered, remembering his own suffering as just an average unknown plebe. "It would be hard on Davy—David—if he makes it."

"So what do you want me to do?"

"Refuse permission," David answered promptly.

But Carrol said, "We don't want anything for Davy that isn't best for him. But what if the medical board doesn't pass him again? The parade might be all he'd ever have. He'd have that to remember at least."

"Suppose we play it by ear," the General answered. "The board meets in April, and it won't fail him after this. But suppose it should, let us say, we still have June week and a hero to honor. Let's leave it that way, shall we?"

"Yes."

Davy's parents answered together, and Mrs. Claybourne leaned over to whisper to Penny, "You can see why we felt we should come. Hubert couldn't stay at that dinner party another minute, because he felt he should leave and do what your father would. He kept pacing around, and finally he came over to me and said, 'It's Dave's boy, and I've made a decision. Do you mind leaving?' and of course, I didn't."

"It was wonderful of you," Penny said, feeling so proud of Davy that she wanted to go out

187

to the kitchen and drag him in by his short wavy hair. "It makes me feel quite emotional to have General Claybourne refer to Davy as 'Dave's boy.' It's a beautiful compliment to Dad."

"Oh, the Colonel is Hubert's idol," Mrs. Claybourne said as she stood up. "And now we really must go. 'Ten minutes,' Hubert told me. 'You're always the timekeeper, so give me the nod when ten minutes are up.' Ten minutes?" She laughed. "Why, he'd sit here all night, chinning with your father." And she said in a soft but authoritative voice, "Hubert. Hubert, dear, I'm ready to leave."

A subdued quiet followed their departure. David poked the dying embers in the fireplace, Carrol stacked ash trays to be emptied, and Penny distributed coats.

"It's a far time from when you borned Davy all alone during the war," she said, stopping beside Carrol. "Remember when we took care of him together? All we wanted was for David to come home and see him. Now all we want is what's best for him. We're bursting with pride because that healthy, beautiful baby didn't let polio stop him. It seems that little Davy has grown up to be David now."

"Yes," Carrol said. "David Parrish the fourth. Do you want me to call him in so you can tell him good-bye?"

"And take him away from a girl? Oh, my soul," Penny scoffed. "What could we tell him that would be worth giving up five minutes of Bitsy to hear? You might say, 'Son, reporters are going to come knocking on our door, but don't let them in.' And 'Davy, dear, West Point was going to give a nice review for you, but we told them not to.' That would thrill him." Penny was buttoning her red coat and turning up the collar. "If I were you, I'd just casually mention that he has a good chance to go to the Point. He won't believe you, but you can tell him anyway."

"Oh, go on home." David had heard her, and he said, "You sound like a bad second-act ending. Josh, get her out of here." But after he had shaken his father's hand in a firm grip, after he had kissed his mother good night, he closed the front door and took Carrol in his arms.

"It's been a big night," he said, resting his cheek against her hair. "Do you remember the night when the doctor came in and told us Davy would live?" He could feel her nod, and he went on, "I cried that night. I'd never thought of doing it all the time Davy was so sick, when we were frightened and praying to keep him, but that night a dam burst. Joy and relief spilled right over the broken dam. I cried."

"I remember, darling." Carrol reached up and touched his eyelids gently. He was always so strong, her David.

"I'm not ashamed to cry," he said. "I might have done it tonight if the folks hadn't been here.

I wanted to put my head right down on the mantel and say, 'Thank you, God. Thank you, thank you, thank you.' It was all I could think of to say. I was so darn proud of Davy. . . ."

"I was too, darling. I am. We always are," Carrol said. "He's no dearer to us than the others, but he's had to work so hard for what he has. There's something—special about Davy."

"Well, he's all right now." David lifted her chin and kissed her. Then he said, squaring his shoulders, "Our little sentimental spell is over, but I'm glad we shared it. We always have, and we always will. Shall we go tell Davy what the General said?"

"Let's wait a few minutes. Somehow," Carrol said thoughtfully, "I have a feeling that he'd rather talk to Bitsy a little while longer than hear he has a good chance to go to the Point. Davy's never one to rush things. Am I right?"

"Right," David answered, and it was exactly what Davy would have said had he heard them.

Sitting at the glass-topped table in the blue-and-white breakfast room, Davy liked looking at Bitsy, who sat at right angles to him. She had pushed the salt and pepper shakers nearer, had fussed over buttering his bread and smearing it with jelly, and was now sitting with her arms crossed on the table, regarding him curiously.

"I've told you twice, Bits," he said, pushing his empty plate away and crossing his own arms, "there wasn't any reason for me to stand around there. I'd brought the guy in, and that's all I could do."

"You could have tried to find out how he was," she argued.

"I *knew* how he was. I'd been with him a darned long time. All he had coming by then was to get a bone set and some tape put around his middle, and he'd be as good as new. My job was finished."

"But suppose it wasn't." She studied him carefully, wondering why she had ever felt sorry for Davy. Why she had considered him too young, and too much in need of her sympathy and understanding to feel romantic about him? He was always about; and when he wasn't, she didn't miss him. Or at least, she hadn't. It's only hero worship, she told herself. Davy was still Davy. So she continued crossly, "Suppose Vance hadn't figured out who you were? How would they ever have known?"

"No need to." He grinned at her then and said, "There wasn't any reward out for the guy— no five-thousand-dead-or-alive sort of thing—and anyway, Deering would have remembered and called me up sometime. I don't see what you're in such a stew about."

"The parade," she told him. "Parri said they're going to give you a parade. Don't you want it?"

"Parri's a nut," he answered, shrugging. "She's

got an imagination that ties her mother's. West Point doesn't hand out parades the way the Boy Scouts give out merit badges."

"But would you like one?"

"Who knows?" Davy exchanged his empty plate for one that held a square of cake hidden under a mound of whipped cream, and said, hunting around for a fork, "Unaccustomed as I am to getting the VIP treatment, I can't imagine it. I'm not the kind of guy, Bits, that crowds stand up and cheer for. I'm just not, and you ought to know it by now. Here, have a bite of cake."

He held out the fork, but Bitsy pushed it away. "David Parrish," she said, wishing she felt toward him as she had even so late as that afternoon, "you make me tired. You don't care the least little bit about what people think of you."

"I care what *you* think." Davy laid his free hand over hers and looked soberly at her. "If it would please you," he said, "I'd stand up like an astro chimp and let a dozen parades march past me. You don't know what a lift it gave me to find you were still waiting here."

"You didn't act like it," she retorted, knowing she was pouting, but enjoying it.

"What did you want me to do, leap at you and kiss you? Jump up and down and say, 'Oh, goody, goody, goody, Bitsy's here?' I'm not that type either."

"You could be if you'd let yourself go."

"I might."

He attacked his cake again, and Bitsy decided that their romantic love scene, all four short speeches of it, was over. Then he unexpectedly looked up and said, "Maybe I could at that. Want I should kiss you now?"

"Oh, don't be silly."

This bantering was getting them nowhere. Davy had not kissed her. He had not considered a review in his honor with even normal seriousness. He was simply forking up cake again. "I think I should go home," she said. And she added with withering sarcasm, "If your horse can spare you, that is."

"What's Sing got to do with it?" he asked.

His napkin had slipped to the floor, so he was under the table when she answered, "Just that I haven't my car and you'll have to drive me."

"Okay." Her little foot looked pretty from down there, tapping away in its high-heeled sandal, but he came up and said, "Wait till I go in and tell Mom and Dad." Then he looked up and saw his parents standing in the doorway. "Hi," he said, with a great feeling of relief. He couldn't go on irritating Bitsy forever, so he urged, "Come on in and join us."

CHAPTER 12

Even by hurrying as fast as they could, the morning was half gone before Parri and Barbie reached Gladstone.

Barbie's mother had hurried too, leaving her housework undone in order to deliver them at Round Tree Farm by nine o'clock, and they had gone rushing in to find Minna the only one at home.

"Where's Mums?" Parri asked, flying into the kitchen where Minna sat having a peaceful breakfast.

"She took Joshu to Scout meeting."

"Then where's Daddy?"

"He's gone to the city, and John's gone to the lumber yard to buy some fence posts," Minna said placidly, spooning sugar into her coffee cup. "Your mother said she'd be back in an hour, and for you to sit down and not fuss."

"Oh, dear!" Parri flopped into a chair and groaned. "We can't wait an hour!" she cried. "We have to be at Davy's right *now!*" And she swung around to call, "Barbie, come out here. What are we going to do?"

"What about?" Barbie appeared in the doorway from the long side hall, still carrying her suitcase. Her light curls were neatly brushed, in contrast to Parri's flyaway locks that were rising higher and higher as she pushed her hands frantically through them. She wore her nylon stockings that were reserved for parties and Sundays, as did Parri, and her new green coat. "Has something else happened?" she asked, putting her suitcase down.

"*Happened!* We're stuck here, that's what!" Parri shrieked. "Run, stop your mother."

"She's gone."

"So's everyone else. How," Parri asked miserably, "are we going to get to Gladstone? The reporters will all be there by now, and they're probably taking Davy's picture, and Sing's, and they might even take ours if we could get there in time. How are we going to do it?"

"I don't know," Barbie said helplessly. And she suggested without much enthusiasm, "We might walk."

"Two miles? It would take forever." Gloom settled over Parri like soot, and she slumped down in her chair. It was unfair to have got this far and be stopped, just because Joshu had been on the spot to be taken somewhere before she was. He could have gone on his bicycle. And then she sprang up. "*We'll* go on the bikes!" she cried. "You can ride mine and I'll ride Joshu's. You know how to ride a bike, don't you?"

"Of course." Barbie looked down at her nylons that sprang runs at the touch of a fingernail, and feared what bicycle pedals would do to them. "I don't think I want to," she began dubiously, but Parri was already flying out the door that led into the garage.

"Here," she said, straining to lift her own blue two-wheeler from the hooks that suspended it from the ceiling. "Take it. If the tires are sort of soft, it doesn't matter."

Joshu's racer was easier to roll out, since he used it every day and it sat on the floor, but its handlebars were turned down in flat, racing position. "Oh, gosh," she said, crouching over them and preparing to push off, "I don't think I can see where I'm going. You'd better start first, so I can follow you, but watch out for icy spots in the road."

"But I don't know where Gladstone is," Barbie protested, one leg through the frame of her own mount and looking down on tires that seemed awfully flat on the bottom.

"Why, just go to the crossroad and then straight right in a sort of curving-around way," Parri said, rising up to point. "You drove over there with Mose and Jake and me last week."

"But I didn't pay attention to where we went." Barbie put her other foot down and stood up. "Let's telephone somebody to come get us," she suggested.

"And waste valuable time? Don't be silly." Parri was already headed for the garage doorway, and she called back, "We can be there by the time anyone could get here for us. Come on, I'll lead."

They went along the driveway and turned onto the asphalt road without mishap. Parri, horizontal as she had to be, was positioned to see any glaze in the road and circle it. Barbie, close behind, was not so fortunate. Only a wild leap saved her from taking a spill. "I don't like it," she said, watching her bicycle skid off into the ditch. "I don't want to meet reporters looking all awful. You can ride and I'll walk."

It took Parri several minutes of valuable time to persuade her to get back on the bicycle again, and she did it only by promising, "We'll go straight along the dry part in the middle, and if I see something coming I'll wigwag to you."

Parri was a country girl and she knew her roads.

Furthermore, the bicycle had been her means of transportation for as many years as she had been able to sit on its saddle and steer it. However, by the time they had pumped along the winding driveway into Gladstone, she did admit to herself that she had never undertaken such a long journey on such a cold day. Her eyes stung from the icy wind, her ears burned like fire, and even constant sniffing hadn't kept her nose from dripping. "Golly," she said, letting her bicycle fall against the terrace steps and holding out her arms to stop Barbie, who was bumbling along on a flat tire, "I don't see how Davy ever stayed out two or three hours on a horse."

"He didn't have to pump," Barbie said, feeling in her pocket for a cleansing tissue, "and he didn't fall off all the time." Then she became aware of something Parri had failed to notice. There were no cars in the driveway. "Where are all the reporters?" she asked.

"Oh, mercy, don't tell me we've missed it after all! I can't stand it!"

Parri pulled Barbie up the steps with her and tugged open the massive front door without waiting for Perkins to come out of his little office beside it. She knew where to find her aunt, if not Davy, so took several turns along a corridor and stopped in the doorway of a small pretty morning room where Carrol Parrish did her accounts and business correspondence. "Good morning, Aunt

Carrol," she said, still breathing hard from her ride. "Here's Barbie. We're looking for Davy. Do you know where he is?"

"Now, where do you think?" Carrol laid down her pen and smiled at them. "Come in," she said. "Davy's out in the stable. Hello, Barbie."

"Have the reporters all gone?" Parri demanded, while Barbie tried to shake loose from her captor.

"Reporters?" Carrol shook her head and looked through the window glass as if trying to see the stable through the stone bulk of the garage. "Why, I don't know," she said. "I've been so busy answering the telephone that if anyone asks specifically for Davy, I simply transfer the call back to him. A syndicate did call—I forget which one —and Perkins said a young man came in a car and he had 'dispatched' him on to Davy."

"We'll see you later. Come on, Barbie."

They hurried along another corridor, still linked together, but at the open door to a powder room Barbie jerked free. "I will not go out there looking like a goon," she declared. "I'm going to wash my hands and face, and comb my hair, and put on a little lipstick, so you'll just have to wait."

"All right." Parri caught a glimpse of herself in the big mirror lining one whole side of the powder room and decided she too needed some repair work. She looked worse than Barbie, so she opened a drawer in a small French dressing table and brought out brushes and combs and several shades of new lipsticks. "Choose whichever one of these you want and keep it," she said, opening the lipsticks and setting them upright in a row.

"Keep it? Why?"

"Because the idea around here is that if you need something, you need it. Nobody wants to use a secondhand lipstick."

"Well, of all things."

Barbie was thoughtful while they hurriedly made themselves presentable again; and as they picked their way along a brick walk that led through a garden where bushes were wrapped in burlap, she said, "It must be wonderful to be so rich. Don't you ever feel uncomfortable when you come here?" she asked. "But you wouldn't, of course, because you're rich too."

"Oh, we aren't rich," Parri told her, remembering the uproar a seven-hundred-and-fifty-dollar coat had caused. "I guess Mums and Daddy do make a lot of money, but Daddy's always putting it back in another play. He makes investments sometimes, because he says he doesn't want us all to go broke if he should. Why, I don't get as big an allowance as you do."

"No, I guess you don't," Barbie answered, finding comfort in that. It had secretly worried her, because she preferred going to Parri's house rather than having Parri come to hers. Her father was only a lawyer and her mother only president of the PTA, while Parri's parents were celebrities. There was such a sparkle in going to Round Tree Farm and looking at them at close range, and she hadn't realized until now that they economized like everyone else. "But Davy's rich," she said. "It's too bad you can't grow up and marry him some day."

"Maybe you can do it," Parri answered, grinning. "He's crazy about Bitsy Jordon now, but I don't see how *three* Parrishes can marry *three* Jordons. It just couldn't happen, that's all, so you be nice to Davy. Or Lang," she added, watching Lang come out of the stable, then go back in. And she clutched Barbie's arm. "There's a car there," she cried, "and it doesn't belong to anybody I know! Oh, Barbie, *hurry!*"

Lang had appointed himself Davy's manager. He was the one who answered the telephone calls. He was the one who said, "Sure, come on out," while Davy went on applying liniment to Sing's sore foot. He was the one who had built up Davy's brief story to the AP reporter, and had shooed off the boy who had wanted an interview for his high school newspaper. He had taken on the job of keeping out all the local photographers who wanted to snap pictures, in the hope of selling one to the syndicates, and had promised the well-known county photographer, Snap Holt, exclusive rights to the New York papers.

This was too small a deal, his acute business sense told him, for the big boys to bother with sending out a camera crew, so he had done everything in a way that would best put Davy in the news. His family often wondered if Lang loved anyone but himself. He could have told them he did. He loved Davy and looked up to him. He didn't want to be like Davy, but there were times when he wanted to borrow a few of Davy's virtues.

"Well, look who's here," he said, as Parri and Barbie came from the cold gray light into semidarkness. And he grinned at Barbie. "Don't tell me you're wanting an interview for old HFHS," he said.

"No." Barbie had seen Lang only once, when she had come to Gladstone to pick up Parri, and his dark presence in the hall had awed her. He had looked so cold and haughty. She couldn't know it was because of his amazing resemblance to his mother's father, for whom he was named—a man who had parlayed a small fortune to fabulous wealth, yet had been warm and shy with those he loved. "I just came for the excitement," she said, "but there doesn't seem to be any."

"There will be," he told her. "Deering's tac is in with old Dave now. A tac in the tack room, get it?" Then he took special note of Parri, "Hi, Pug," he said, speaking slightingly of her nose, which was neither short nor long, like her mother's. "We've got a committee of three cadets coming, so mind your manners."

"What three cadets?" Parri asked.

"From *The Pointer*. They're upperclassmen, so don't get your hopes up."

"But why can't we go in and see Davy?" It was all very well to be met by Lang, who was something like the stage manager in one of her mother's plays, but she had come to meet the star of the show. "We came to tell Davy how proud we are of him," she said. "Why can't we talk to him, even if a tac is in there? He isn't incommunicado, is he?"

"Big word." Lang grinned at her, but said, "Listen, Pug. You don't interfere with the military—not when Davy's set his heart on getting into the Point. This is his deal, and even I'm staying out. Lord knows why he wants it—I wouldn't, but he does—so lay off. I suppose you know General Claybourne came to see the folks last night and told them Davy's got a good chance . . ."

"Oh, thank goodness!" Parri interrupted.

". . . of passing his physical," Lang went on, unperturbed. "So either sit down or scram."

"Well—gracious me," she said. She had lost contact with her vocabulary, so she sat down on a scarred bench and yanked Barbie down beside her. "We'll sit here all day if we have to." But thinking of the way she had hurried, of the biting wind and cold she had endured to get here, she asked, "Won't there be any more pictures?"

"There haven't been any, yet," Lang said, grinning. "Sing's still standing with his foot in a bucket of water and looks like the deuce. Davy looks worse because he's got on a sweatshirt and old jeans. You can trot up to the house and get him some clothes if you want to. I started to, then got afraid to leave him. How about it?"

"Oh, dear." It was so unsafe to go away. The cadets might come. Davy might emerge and take them back into the tack room with him and she would be left outside holding his clothes. Or it might give her an excuse to barge in with the armload like an angel of mercy. Parri was undecided.

"I'll go," Barbie offered. "I'm not supposed to be here, really, so I'll go up and get whatever clothes you want, if someone up there knows what they are and can find them for me."

"I'll drive you." Lang looked from Barbie to Parri, who didn't inspire him with her dependability. Could she keep guard on the bench? Would she have sense enough to know who was who and who wasn't? A high school reporter would look better to her than the bearded photographer he expected, and she was quite apt to inform Davy of what was in store for him, and so scare him off. He knew he should take her and leave Barbie, but he didn't want to. "Now, look," he said. "If you hear Davy and Captain Reimer open the door to come out, you scoot. Go back and stay in one of the stalls."

"Yes, sir." Parri had no intention either of scooting or hiding. Davy was her cousin just as much as he was Lang's brother, and she had his interest just as much at heart as Lang did. She would help him if she got the chance. "Okay," she said acceptantly. "If anyone comes, I'll make him sit down out here." And she added silently, "After I've announced him. I'll see that Davy takes each one in turn, and I'll stand by like a secretary."

"We'll be back in fifteen minutes," Lang said, knowing he shouldn't trust her, but unable to resist going off with as cute a girl as Barbie. "I'm sure Captain Reimer won't come out before I get back because he just went in, but remember what I told you. Let Davy walk out to his car with him. *Alone,*" he added.

"Roger. Over and out."

Parri leaned back on her bench and watched them go out a small door cut in one of the big double ones and close it behind them. She could have told Lang that he wouldn't be driving Barbie because he had no car, but he might turn around and come back. It seemed wiser to let him find it out for himself and start walking. It would take him longer that way.

She wished she had a telephone. The house phone hung on the wall above her head, but the outside line was in with Davy. It didn't matter, she consoled herself, because she had nothing new to report to her friends, except that she was sitting alone in a cold, drafty barn. She couldn't hear what was being said in the tack room, not even when she got up and pressed her ear against the door; so, stamping her feet to find out if she had any blood at all left in them, she went over to look out through a small front window. Nothing outside. Nothing at all could she see while she stood stamping her feet. Nothing.

And then, when surely five of her fifteen precious minutes were gone, she saw a car coming. It was a taxicab, and it bumped its way over the frozen ruts in the lane that led to the stable and the barns. Would it turn in here or go on? It— it turned. Parri almost ran out to meet it. Only her love of the dramatic held her still, and she watched three cadets get out. Oh, joy, she thought, and hoped her nose wasn't still red.

They wore their beautiful gray overcoats with the capes turned back, and even in the dull December daylight their brass buttons shone. and one was short, and the tall one was as blond They wore gray caps also, and two were tall as Davy.

"Wow!" she said, and ran back to sit down again.

Cold air rushed at her as they opened the small door and came in; and knowing they were as blinded in the gloom as she had been, she stood up and said in her best secretarial voice, "Good morning. May I help you?"

"Oh, hello." The blond cadet could either see better than the others or was spokesman for the trio. "We're from *The Pointer*," he said, taking off his cap in such a polite way that Parri almost sat down again from surprise.

They all snatched off their caps while she blinked at them, but he was the one who went on, "We came to see David Parrish. Is he around?"

"Yes, but he's—he's in conference now," Parri answered, copying the way her father's secretary did it. Then she grinned, and pointing over her shoulder with her thumb, she said, "He's in there. He's got an officer with him."

"We'd better wait."

They smiled sociably at her, and the short one said, "I'm Bart Selby. Royce Linninger here, and our first classman and spokesman, Elliott Ferguson."

"I'm Parrish MacDonald," Parri answered, "but everyone calls me Parri. I've been left in charge, and I don't know what to do now."

"Why don't we all sit down and be patient?" Elliott was the one to take up the conversation again, and with a little crowding together they managed to share the bench with her.

It was much warmer with gray overcoats pressed against her, but it was uncomfortable,

207

too. Not physically, but mentally. Parri, as hostess, could think of nothing to say. She looked at first one, then another, sitting stiffly erect beside her, and finally she blurted out, "You'd better put your caps back on. It's freezing cold in here. I never knew horses liked it so cold."

"Are you cold?"

Three heads turned, and a West Point cap was clapped over her curls. "Oh, thank you," she said, peeking out from under the visor to see who had put it there. She was relieved to find the good-looking first classman still holding his, as was the short one who had said he was Bart Selby. "Thank you, Mr. Linninger," she said, and sent him a pleased smile. "I never wear a hat," she went on honestly, "and my head isn't a bit cold, but this is fun. I feel so—cadetish."

They laughed so companionably with her that she was further encouraged to say, "If I were a boy, I'd want to go to the Point. It's all Davy—David talks about. But I suppose you know he can't get in."

"Why not?"

Two small notebooks and stubby pencils had been produced from somewhere—from the two caps she wasn't wearing, she saw—so she took off the one she had on and let its owner feel around in the band. "Why, because he had polio when he was little," she said, with the cap back on. "Poor David. He can't pass his physical."

The pencils were scribbling away. The faster she talked, the faster they wrote, and it took very few pertinent questions to keep her going. Davy was getting a sob story that, if printed, would wring the hardest heart on a medical board. And by the time she had reached the place to say, "He walks miles every day, and he has a special gym, and swims and rides, and made his athletic letter at Claymore Academy, but they still won't pass him because his legs don't match," the editor and his staff had enough notes to fill three columns. They had far more than they could ever have wrung out of a fellow who was too shy to be thanked.

"Thanks a lot," Elliott said, snapping his notebook shut. "You've been a terrific help. We'll have to get back now."

"But David should be out in a minute," she said, suddenly appalled by what she had done, especially as she watched silent signals for departure pass across her and felt the cap leave her head. "He'd be so proud to meet you."

"Our taxi's meter is ticking away," Elliott said, "and we're due back before mess call. So suppose you tell Parrish we were here and one of us will see him later. Okay?"

"Well, I guess so," Parri said doubtfully, wishing Lang would come back and tell her what to do or say next. Had she ruined Davy by talking too much? Had she wrecked an interview that

209

might be important to him? "He'll be awfully disappointed," she said inadequately.

"Oh, we'll see him," Bart Selby promised. "Tomorrow's Sunday, and we'll have some time off then." And he asked, "Do you happen to have a picture of Parrish around?"

"No, but his mother has," Parri answered, feeling that their asking for a photograph was a good sign they were planning to print some of the things she had told them about him. And she added hopefully, "If you could wait a little while, a news photographer is coming out to take some pictures of him for the New York papers. The syndicates want to write about him for nation-wide coverage."

"We'll try to get one of those, and we'll stop at the house, too," Elliott said; and she gave a gasp of dismay.

Lang was up there. Lang would murder her far more completely than her mother ever had for all her threatening, and if he didn't finish the job, Davy would. "I think you'd better wait and ask a real photographer for one," she said, as they all stood up. "A glossy reproduces better," she told them, as the daughter of an actress and producer would know. "I'd be glad to bring it to you, and anyway, I don't think anybody's at home now."

"Okay. We'll call up Snap Holt and see what he's got." She had been a blessing out of the blue to them, so Royce Linninger added, "Thanks a lot,

Parri. We've already talked to Deering and he praised David to the skies. We'll make a good story for him, so don't you worry." And because he was the youngest, he asked, "Do you ever drag at the Point?"

"Mercy, no, not yet," Parri told him frankly. "I'm only a freshman in high school." She thought high school sounded much more impressive than a girl's school, so said it quickly. "My mother used to, though," she added. "But of course her brother was there—David's father, you know—and he sort of looked after her. David won't be there to look after me if you and General Claybourne don't get busy and help him." She smiled hopefully at them, and simultaneously and in a blinding flash it dawned on each of them who she was.

"She's Penny Parrish's daughter," they said in a chorus, having fallen over each other to get outside the narrow door, and Elliott Ferguson added, "Boy, what a subcaption: 'Parrish MacDonald, daughter of the actress, Penny Parrish, praises hero cousin.' Wow. Big splash. I wish we had a picture of her with her mother."

"I wish I had a picture of *her*," Royce said, looking back at the stable. "It would sure look good on my locker door."

"Wait till next year." Elliott shoved him into the taxi after Bart and crowded in on the end. They had far more material than they had hoped to get; and, safely engaged to a girl whom he hoped to marry in June, Elliott was already through with Parri. "Step on it, Bill," he ordered the driver, a man accustomed to waiting an endless time for cadets, then driving at breakneck speed to get them back for some crazy formation they didn't dare miss.

From her window, Parri watched the taxi leave. She was thankful Davy hadn't appeared to hear her blasting off at full steam; but when the door opened and he followed Captain Reimer out, she felt her knees buckle. Davy looked happy almost to the point of lunacy, she thought—as if he were seeing visions. As if he were seeing himself in a fine officer's uniform, bundled up in an overcoat and muffler. Then she sneaked another cautious peek at him and decided he didn't look that way at all. He looked pleased but skeptical. But whichever way he looked, she decided unhappily, his expression was going to take a sudden change when he found out his young cousin had lost an important interview for him. To delay the awful moment, she flattened herself against the window, trying to look as if a poster of a girl had been pasted there.

"He's a swell guy," Davy said, closing the door after his guest and discovering her. "Where did Lang go?"

"Up to the house to get you some clothes to wear for the pictures," Parri answered, after having swallowed three times.

"Crazy kid." Davy grinned and said, "Snap was here while Lang was eating his breakfast. I forgot to tell him."

"Oh, Davy." Parri was disgusted with her hero. Both she and Lang had tried to do so much for him, and he'd already had his picture taken, looking like a hobo. "Lang wanted you to look nice," she said fretfully.

"Well, Snap liked it this way. I offered to slick up, but he wanted me in Sing's stall, taking care of my trusty horse. He said it was a better news angle," Davy said with a shrug, "but I couldn't care less. Pictures aren't going to get me into the Academy, Parri. It'll be a good leg or a bum one that will make the final decision. Ballyhoo won't do it, and that's what I told Captain Reimer. He agrees with me, by the way, so I'm not going to see anyone else. No cadets, no anyone. I'll play it straight."

Oh, mercy. What to say? *The Pointer* had Davy's life story, practically from birth, and he was sure to see it. "Well, dear me," Parri said, hoping all the linotype machines in West Point would break down, that the editorial staff would file away her interview as too drippy to print, that her mother and father would suddenly decide to go around the world and take her with them. "I guess you know what you're doing."

"I most certainly do."

He started back to Singing Star's stall, but

Parri stopped him by asking, "Is it all right if I sit in the tack room and get warm? I have to wait for Barbie and Lang to come back."

"Is Barbie with Lang?" Davy turned around and shook his head as if he were sorry for her. "You've got a long wait, kid," he said. "You get warm while I change Sing's bandage, then I'll walk up to the house with you."

"But, Davy, I don't think I want you to." She was afraid to be alone with him. She never could keep still about anything, so what if she should start talking about the cadets?

"And if any more cadets come around," he said, just as if he had read her thoughts, "tell them I've gone to New York. Captain Reimer and I saw some come and leave, but I didn't know you were out here. Did you see them?"

"Yes, and, oh Davy, I told them some terrible things. Davy," she cried out in misery, "I told them you used to be lame!"

"I don't doubt it." His gaze was so level that she cringed. Then he smiled and came back. "Don't worry about it," he said, giving her a rough, warming slap on the back. "Reimer's going to tell them exactly how much they can print. Any stuff you told them won't make any difference, one way or the other."

"It won't?"

"Of course not."

She thought it sad. Nobody would read about

poor baby Davy learning to walk in braces; poor older Davy swimming back and forth in a pool at Hot Springs; poor grown Davy tramping weary miles, riding hours on end, and chasing a tennis ball. People should be given the chance to read about how brave he was. Oh, they should, they should. "Are you *really* sure?" she asked.

"I told you I am." He was a little angry with her for standing there with her head down, looking so gosh-darned miserable, but he only said, "Forget it. I'll go up to the house with you and have some lunch. I can come back and fix Sing up later." And then, in pure exasperation, he took her by the arm and shook her gently as he said, "Oh, Parri, for Pete's sake, stop *crying!*"

CHAPTER 13

THE MONTHS SLIPPED BY. Christmas had come and gone, bringing Parri a new red coat that surpassed her wildest dreams. It was full and had a swing, yet was youthful; and as she modeled it for the family, it reminded her of April. April was happy, she knew, because a pretty little ingenue had left the cast of *Delayed Honeymoon* and April had been given the small part.

She and April owed their whole wondrous present to a red coat, Parri reflected again, when it was late in the month whose name April had chosen. It was Sunday afternoon, and she was sitting on the front steps of Gladstone as she usually did, waiting for some of her gang to come pick her up. She wore her new powder-blue Easter suit with its short, boxy jacket, and held her white leather car coat on her lap. A bright red cardinal cavorting about in a tree had reminded her of the red coat, and the coat had reminded her of April.

I was such a stupe then, she thought, watching some fussy sparrows chase the cardinal and a gentle robin out of the budding tree. All I did was moan and groan and want to grow up. How could Mums and Daddy know I was lonesome if I hadn't sense enough to tell them so?

And those thoughts, for some reason, took her skittering mind on to Davy. How could Davy know that Bitsy Jordon had a date if she didn't go out to the stable and tell him? "Oh, darn," she said. And then she added, "Poor Davy," and went down the steps and followed the driveway around the house.

Jake would drive back to the stable to find her. Barbie, or Dicky-Wicky, or someone would remind him that they sometimes picked her up out there; and since the gathering of the gang was to be at her house today, she was sure they wouldn't go off and leave her. She had allowed herself a full half hour in which to sit alone in the sunshine and dream, so she picked her careful way along the spongy gravel that began beyond the garage.

Davy was exactly where she expected him to be, saddling up in the runway; and when she stood beside Singing Star, she plunged right in and said, "Uncle Bobby just told us that Keith Drayton is over at Bitsy's."

"So what?" Davy gave her a hard, cold stare

217

as he jerked the girth on his saddle tighter and made Singing Star grunt. "What's it to you?" he asked.

"Why, nothing—I guess," she answered, moving away from Sing's lips when they nipped at her new suit's pocket for sugar. "I just thought you ought to know it."

"So I know it." David dropped the saddle skirt and led the horse away and tied him to the ring in the post. "Parri," he said sternly, coming back, "I think you and I had better have a talk. Let's sit outside on the bench."

"All right." She followed him meekly out into the sunshine, wondering what was to come.

He had forgiven her for the dramatic story *The Pointer* had published in spite of Captain Reimer's protests, and had even agreed with his father that its reprint in the newspapers might have helped him get his appointment. "At least it didn't wreck me," he had said when he forgave her, which wasn't until the medical board had pronounced him physically fit. But she didn't like to remember the months in between: the worried, awful months when she was sure she had ruined his chances. Some of the time she hadn't thought too much about it, being so excited and busy with her new life and new school, but at every Sunday family gathering she had tried to be wherever Davy wasn't. Until last week. Last week he had received official confirmation of his appointment, and now she was his busy little helper again. She really was a great help to Davy, she told herself. She was almost like a good-luck charm.

"The seat looks sort of dusty," she mentioned hesitantly, stopping before the bench along the stable wall, where Davy and Lang often sat to clean their equipment; so Davy took off his riding jacket and spread it out for her to sit on.

"Heaven knows why I bother with you," he said, sitting down beside her and looking off into the distance as if hoping to find the answer somewhere in the rim of blue sky above the trees. "I swear I won't, and then I do. You're always causing me trouble."

"Why? I mean, how?" Parri was curious as well as chastened. Their ideas about her seemed to differ. So she prodded, "What have I done to upset you?"

"First it was that darned coat. I advised you to pay for it, and you moped about it."

"I didn't mope," she protested, knowing she had.

"And then I tried to find dates for you and April, and Mom blew up at me because I went home and said you weren't getting a fair shake from your folks."

"Maybe that helped me get it," she praised.

"And then there was this last stupid business of . . ."

"I've said I'm sorry about that, Davy."

"I know. But if I hadn't held forth to you about how sunk I was not to go to the Point, you might

219

not have got mixed up in it. You're a good kid, Parri," he said, turning to look at her, "but suppose you lay off me for a while. With Bitsy, I mean. Let me handle that without your help."

"But are you?"

"I am. I've got into the Academy, and it's going to take me four years to get out. I'm not any girl's dream boy right now. Bitsy knows it, and she's free to date. We've talked it out, and we both understand."

"That's good. And anyway," Parri said, bouncing back because they were on a different subject, "three Parrishes couldn't possibly marry three Jordons. I told Barbie that. Bitsy'll be too old by the time you're a lieutenant, so maybe Barbie will be just right. I'd sort of promised Lang to her, but I think I'd rather have her wait for you."

"Oh, gosh." Davy wished a rattling old jalopy would come puffing along the driveway, but he said, "Now you listen. You're to keep your mind on your own age group. I'm fond of you, Parri, but you've been a constant pain to me for a good many years. Ever since I had to wear the leg braces you blabbed about, and had to play with you because you were little and couldn't knock me down, I've had you stuck to me. I suppose I've felt protective, but you're on your own now. Get it?"

"It's going to be awful," she said, sighing. "I'll be so alone. Did you know that Mums has decided to do the new play Daddy wants to produce for her?"

"I heard something about it."

"She's panicked. She's the most scared-cat actress there ever was, but she says she has to do it. She hasn't been on TV, or in the movies, or even done a play for two years, so the columnists keep starting rumors about her, and she has to. It nearly kills her to think of leaving Joshu and me out here alone, especially since I have so many friends scattered around and go in town to high school."

"Oh, she won't leave you alone." Davy knew Penny would stay in the town apartment two nights a week, when she had Wednesday and Saturday matinees, and would be home every afternoon but one when Parri came from school. He had heard it discussed often enough, goodness knows, with endless arrangements being made for John to drive Parri wherever she wanted to go, for either his grandmother or his mother to take over until his Uncle Josh could hustle out from New York. "Parri," he said, "rehearsals don't even start until early fall."

"I know it, and you'll be in the Point by then. But do you know the one good thing about it?" Parri slid around on the bench and grinned at him, when she had meant to stay looking sad and forlorn. "I'll be fifteen by then," she said, as Davy didn't answer. "Mums is going to take a whole row of seats on my fifteenth birthday and

221

let me give a theater party. Daddy's going to take us all to dinner somewhere before the play, and we're going to have ice cream and cake in Mum's dressing room afterward, and then they'll bring us all home. Oh, I wish you were going to be there, Davy."

"I don't." Davy knew he sounded gruff and unappreciative, so he patted her hand and added, "We'll all go in to watch your mother some afternoon, you and Lang and Joshu and Carli and I. I'd like it better that way."

"So would I, if the show doesn't fail. You know," she said wistfully, "it's awful, but I sort of wish it would. We could go back to being a normal family then. I love it when Mums stays home and bakes cookies that even Blitz can't eat."

"You wouldn't like it if you didn't have money to buy the cookie mix with." Davy did see a car approaching at last, coming bumpity-bump on its antiquated springs, and he got up and pulled Parri to her feet. "Now you remember what I told you," he warned. "Keep out of my business, Parri. I mean it."

"I will," she promised. And then, as if the whole conversation had never taken place, she asked, "You really aren't going over to Bitsy's?"

"I told you I'm not."

"It seems sort of sad," she said. "A beautiful girl and a hero."

"Parri!"

"Excuse me. I forgot, but I'll remember next time." She felt so lighthearted. She felt as happy and full of promise as the spring bursting out around her. "You know something?" she said, as the car stopped beyond the cobblestones and gave a timid squawk of its horn. "I feel as if life's just beginning for both of us."

It was always beginning for her, or ending, or falling apart in the middle, Davy reflected, just as it was for her mother. He was glad he had calm, well-adjusted parents. But even so he was eager to see what Parri, in her own odd environment, would make of herself. She had such a fiery imagination and such a great capacity for love that he hoped she wouldn't go off the deep end and throw them away. Like falling in love with someone as dopey as that wacky Wicky-Dicks, or whatever the grinning idiot's name was. Parri was— she was something special, he told himself, looking down at her, so dressed up and young. She had something. "Okay," he said. "Life's just beginning. I'll make a bargain with you."

"What?" she asked, curious but wary.

"I'll keep in touch with you after I'm in the Point if you'll promise to keep right on coming to me with your problems, before they get really big."

"Oh, I will," she cried, "if I ever have any more!" The horn tooted again, louder this time, and she nodded her head up and down to say she was coming. "I don't have any at the moment," she said, searching for one, "unless you count that selfish Natalie making such a play for Mose that he's afraid to even speak to any of the rest of us. I like Mose because he was so good to me when I needed someone to help me; and if you're sure you aren't going to be unhappy about Bitsy, I can stop worrying about that and can devote some of my time to Mose. I may even ask your advice about him."

"I'll be at your service. Right here in my office."

"Silly." Parri started off. She even got as far as putting her foot on a high running board and saying, "Hi, Jake. Hi, Barbie. My goodness, Lang, I didn't expect to see *you*." Then she stepped off and came tearing back.

"Oh, Davy," she cried, looking up at him, her eyes shining, "aren't we happy? Isn't everything just too wonderful for words? You've got West Point and I've got high school! We've got everything we want, so isn't it simply practically perfect?"

"Yes," Davy answered, knowing she had used the one expression that best suited their present and future. "It sure is," he added fervently. And he walked back to the car with her.